RESOLUTION

HEAVEN'S REJECTS MC #5

AVELYN PAIGE

TRIGGER WARNINGS

This book contains graphic scenes of violence, crude language, violence against women, prison, discussion about abortion, and other dark elements.

BLURB

All she wants is him. All he wants is her freedom.

Ginny Azzo has never had an easy life, but for the first time, she's truly happy with where she is. Her focus is on her future with the man she loves, despite her older brother's disapproval.

Lucas "Slider" Sterling spent four years behind bars for the Heaven's Rejects MC. Now he's out and ready to start his life with Ginny. But the danger's not over, and Slider will have to make a choice.

His club or her freedom.

How much is he willing to sacrifice for the woman he loves?

Dedication

To all my patient readers,

I dedicate this book to you, my beloved procrastinators, who have waited a five years for its arrival.

I'd like to apologize for the delay, but let's be honest, life happened. I blinked, and suddenly it was half a decade later. I may be five years late, I've come bearing a book that has been marinated to perfection. It's aged like fine cheese, matured like a fine wine, and ripened like the best excuse I could come up with. Just remember: it's not about the destination; it's about the ridiculous journey that got us here.

Chapter 1

SLIDER

SIX MONTHS AGO

I'VE BEEN in this cell for four years—one thousand four hundred and sixty days.

The air is a stagnant mix of body odor, sweat, and stale Cheetos.

The walls are gun-metal gray, and the fluorescent lights burn through the night, making it difficult to sleep. The prisoners are lifeless, the guards emotionless. I hear the screams of my neighbors in their cells, trying to rattle the guards or picking fights with other inmates across the cell block.

This sentence I agreed to serve was a decision I've questioned more times than I can count on the hard days when my resolve slips. On those days, I have to remind myself why I chose this life. Why did I decided to protect V and the club?

Ginny.

She was the light in my darkness during my solitary confinement.

V was ready to give himself up to save her and Presley, but I couldn't allow him to do that. The club needed him but didn't need me—an expendable prospect easily replaced.

I took his place.

I took his front-row seat in cement hell.

For Ginny, I'd do this a hundred times over.

As I lay on my cot—which may as well be concrete—staring up at the same cracks in the ceiling, I can't help but think about her. Ginny's the only person who makes me feel alive in this hellhole. She's why I wake up every morning—the thought of her smile pushes me through the day. But now, as the end of my sentence creeps closer, I can't shake the feeling I might lose her too.

Four years and not a single word from her.

No calls.

No letters.

Only torturous radio silence. Her beautiful face becomes more like a fading memory than reality with each passing day. Has she forgotten about me? Has she moved on? The thought of Ginny with another man makes my blood boil, the anger a resentment I can't move past.

Ginny Azzo is mine.

My torment.

My pain.

My resolution.

The first time I saw her, I knew she would be trouble. Her dark hair fell in wild waves around her heart-shaped face, and her eyes were the deepest shade of green I'd ever seen. Even then, as a lowly prospect in the club, I knew I wanted her.

She'd been scared and on the run from the Zezzas. If my imprisonment hadn't sealed their fate, I would have stayed by her side. My only hope is in my sacrifice, Ginny is truly free.

The news from my brothers is sparse when it comes to her—the result of her being placed back into protective custody until the last of the Zezza bastards were put away. With it, the threat to her as a star witness for the federal case against them—she was the one person who was still alive and could attest to their part in the American skin trade and the trail of bodies in their wake. She was the pin on the grenade that blew the Zezza operation apart. Without her testimony, the case was circumstantial at best, according to Voodoo, and not enough evidence to put an end to it. Ginny had to be protected at all costs, even if the thought of her being in protective custody made me uneasy.

A girl like her doesn't belong in a cage, even if it is for her safety. She's made to run free, to laugh, to love, and be with me. The thought of her being locked away is unbearable. I need and crave her so badly, and four years locked away hasn't dulled the flame of my passion for her.

She was vulnerable—so much so that Ginny clung to the first person who cared about her safety who wasn't her brother. She clung to me like I was the only source of air for her lungs. She depended on me, and as I got to know her, I fell hard. I found in her what I had been missing my entire life. *Love.* It was the one thing my family's money couldn't buy me, and I had craved from childhood—someone who could see and accept me for who I am and not some picture-perfect idealization of what a well-off family should be.

Ginny saw through the bullshit and saw the side of me, the real me I had hidden away from even the club. The boy I had left behind the moment I stepped foot into my prison sentence.

Would I recognize the man I've become in prison? Will she?

As I lay there, staring at the ceiling, a sudden sense of foreboding creeps up on me. It starts as a chill at the back of my neck and quickly spreads throughout my entire body, a physical manifestation of the fear that has been gnawing on the edges of my mind for the last several months. What if they never release me? What if the Feds decide to keep me locked up indefinitely? I'd asked to see my lawyer for weeks now, but visiting hours came and went without a summons. No word at all. No calls. I haven't heard from the club in months on top of it.

Has something happened?

I rack my brain. I've stayed on the straight and narrow path, giving the law no reason to extend my sentence. I keep to myself and avoid the infighting within the prison factions. One toe out of line means another day without her and my freedom.

So why the radio silence? Ginny, I understand in a way, but the club? My lawyer? None of that makes sense unless another player has entered the game or the terms are changing.

I bolt upright, sweat-drenched and short of breath. My cot squeaks in protest as I strain for control. The cell is barren and still. Too still. A flood of memories from the outside seep through my mind —Ginny's face, the rumble of Harleys on rides, the smell of gas and leather. Those days once felt endless and free, but now it seems as though they occurred in a different lifetime. The thick walls and iron bars remind me how far removed I am from that life. Time has become meaningless in prison, and each day blends into the next until there is no way to keep track. Even worse than the monotony is the pressure building inside me—something isn't right. If only I could figure out what it is, I might be able to find some peace.

A clang in the distance makes me flinch, and a guard's footsteps echo down the hall. It means nothing on its own, but in this desolate place, any sound is enough to cause alarm. I try to focus on something tangible, anything within reach, while taking deep breaths to calm myself, like the gnarled scars on my knuckles or a design etched into the metal frame of my bedpost.

But nothing works.

Fear builds inside me, ready to be triggered like an avalanche of not knowing what lies ahead or what awaits Ginny out there. A tornado builds and spins faster, twisted with danger and uncertainty.

My thoughts turn back to Ginny. What if something has happened to her? What if she's hurt or worse? I couldn't bear the thought, not after everything we've been through and after everything I've sacrificed for her.

And then, as if the universe is listening to my thoughts, the old guard, whose name I can never remember, taps on my cell. "Mail call." He slips a stack of envelopes tied with a piece of twine through the slot in the door. It falls to the cement floor with a quiet thud before his heavy footsteps disappear down the block behind him.

I scramble over to the pile of mail, my fingers eagerly searching for a familiar script. And there it is —Ginny's handwriting scrawled across the front of an envelope, beckoning me like a siren's song. My heart swells with relief and longing as I tear open the envelope, taking care not to damage her delicate cursive.

Inside, I find a single sheet of paper delicately folded as though she had put great thought into each crease. I inhale deeply, taking in the scent of her perfume that clings to the paper—it smells like vanilla, flowers, and comfort all wrapped together. My eyes scan across the words, eager to hear her voice in my mind after so long. The penmanship is elegant, flowing with curves and loops that make me think of the curve of her hips and how her body felt under my hands the last night we were together— just the two of us in her room at the clubhouse.

"Dear Slider," she writes, and my heart leaps at the sound of her voice in my head.

Chapter 2

GINNY

FIVE MONTHS AGO

"YOU READY FOR THIS?" Callie, my lead attorney, leans over and whispers in my ear.

With a smile, I nod. "More than you can imagine." It had been four years since I tasted freedom— four years of moving from safe house to safe house, constantly on the move to avoid being in one place for too long. After the fiasco in Kentucky, my keepers weren't going to take any chances with their star witness.

"Rigo isn't walking away from this," she promises. A promise we both know is out of our hands. The jury will be the deciding factor—twelve people—men, women, fathers, and mothers. Those twelve people held my freedom in their hands, and they didn't even know it. They had the safety of this country to consider as well. Rigo Zezza's reach had been far before I outed their business dealings. The fame would only make it worse.

Everyone knew who Rigo was—Don of the Zezza family, the most powerful organized crime family in the United States. We'd been waiting for this moment for months, and it had finally arrived. He was the last on the FBI's list and the final name to check off for my freedom.

Gio, my now-deceased ex, was the one who had drawn me into this situation. I wanted to rebel against my brother and his new family with the Heaven's Rejects. That rebellion led me straight to Gio and into the hell I'd been living in for far too long. My brother had taken it upon himself to ensure I'd never be bothered by Gio again. Curiosity gets the best of me every so often, and I find myself tempted to ask where his body is located, but I know Jude will never tell me. It's his way of shielding me like he always had done before I thought I could handle the Zezza family on my own.

"Let's go," one of the agents behind me mutters, his hand pressed to his earpiece. "They're ready for us. Room has been cleared." Pressing his hand to the small of my back, he ushers me into the room. Two more agents lead the way, blocking me from the view of the man who sits to the right at a large wooden table.

With Callie and her team beside me, we make our way into the courtroom, the sea of faces all turning to look at us as we enter. I feel their eyes on me, judging me, but I hold my head high and keep moving. The space behind our table is empty. With a ban on the public, my lawyers insisted my brother was not welcome at the proceedings. Their meaning is crystal clear—the Heaven's Rejects needed to stay away. My association with them could hinder the case. It could give the jury a reason to doubt my testimony if they knew I was related to a member of their notorious motorcycle club.

I had to be above reproach.

Unquestionable and undeniably untainted.

Indisputably alone.

The ring of men herds me to the small table. One of the younger officers pulls out a chair, his eyes cold, professional, and calculating. "Sit," he orders with just enough volume to be heard over the rustling of papers and shifting bodies in seats but not so loud that anyone could have possibly eavesdropped on us. I comply, doing my best to ignore the soreness in my back from being in this hard wooden seat for over eight hours yesterday.

The courtroom is barren but for a few chairs scattered around, and no comfort or paddings provided anywhere. It almost feels like a punishment for having to testify.

I peer over my shoulder. The space behind me is still empty. A sigh leaves my lips before I can stop it. Callie's knowing eyes snap over to me. She reaches out, giving my hand a quick, reassuring squeeze before returning to the stack of papers on the table in front of her. I peer back again. My heart is sinking in the space where *he* should be, where Slider should be next to my brother—the two most important men in my life supporting me in the scariest moment in my life.

I take a deep breath and push away the thought. I can't let myself be distracted with thoughts of Slider or Jude. I need to focus on the task at hand—Rigo Zezza—the man who had taken everything away from me.

The reason I spent the last four years in hiding.

The reason I lost Slider.

The reason I lost my brother.

Rigo had to pay for what he'd done, no matter the cost. I may not be able to get those years back from him or his family, but I could live free knowing his reign of terror is over. Another day alone, isolated, and under guard is a price I am willing to pay to see him put away for good.

The trial had been moved from venue to venue until the FBI was finally granted their request to move to a smaller, private place without the press hoarding their way into the courtroom for Rigo's trial. They'd gone so far as to have the jury sequestered in a private hotel, guarded around the clock by multiple agencies. No one in. No one out. Callie has even mentioned that the judge is sequestered away from his family, who had entered protective custody out of precaution. The FBI and the government pulled out all the stops to keep any chance of this case going in Rigo's favor.

The sound of the judge entering the room brings me out of my thoughts. The bailiff booms out, "All rise!" Everyone in the room shuffles to stand. My heart starts to race as I realize the weight of what's about to happen. The judge takes his seat, and the courtroom falls silent, the only sound heard being the shuffling of papers as everyone prepares for the trial to begin.

"You may be seated," the judge declares.

"Are we ready to proceed with closing arguments?"

"We are," my lawyer responds.

"And the defendant?"

"Ready, Your Honor."

The temptation to peer over at Rigo digs at me,

but I shake it away. No good will come from looking that kind of evil in the face again. I'd done enough of that while on the stand for over a week while being examined and cross-examined about my time with their family.

Rigo's attorney stands, and without thinking, I glance over. Rigo is sitting there, looking straight ahead, his eyes cold and calculating. He's wearing a dark suit, looking like he's stepped out of the pages of a men's magazine. His thick, dark hair is slicked back, revealing sharp cheekbones and a strong jawline. He looks like he's completely at ease, as if he's not facing a lifetime behind bars. He peers over at me. I can't help but feel a twinge of fear deep in my stomach at the sight of his cold, merciless gaze on me, but I keep my head high, determination flooding through me.

I will *not* let him break me.

I grit my teeth and remind myself he's not invincible before I look away. He can still be taken down. The evidence is stacked against him, and the jury will see that. I have to believe justice will be served.

His attorney softly walks to the jury box. His pinstripe suit is tailored to perfection. He places his hand on the outer rim of the box, the hint of a smile cracking at the corner of his mouth from the angle I am sitting.

"Members of this esteemed jury, you've heard many fabricated and wild stories regarding my client, Rigo Zezza, over the last few weeks. Outrageous and egregious accounts of theft, corruption, and deception. Accounts that my client has been wrongfully accused of."

I narrow my eyes at Rigo's attorney, feeling anger boiling inside me. How dare he try to make it seem like Rigo's innocent? On what authority should he spin the truth this way to protect such a vile human being? I clench my fists but force myself to take deep breaths to calm down before I make a scene. *Keep it together, Ginny.*

"But the truth is, ladies and gentlemen of the jury… the prosecution has *not* provided you with one shred of concrete evidence to prove Rigo's guilt beyond a reasonable doubt." The attorney pauses, a smug look on his face. "They have only presented circumstantial evidence, hearsay, and the testimony of an… at best, unreliable witness."

My heart sinks, knowing he's referring to me. I take a deep breath, trying not to let his words get to me.

"But I implore you, members of the jury, to use your critical-thinking skills. To consider that just because someone says something is true, does not make it true." He pauses, looking around the room before fixing his gaze on me. "Especially someone who has a history of lying and deceit. A scorned lover seeking revenge for a broken heart."

I feel a blush creeping up my neck, knowing he's referring to my past with the Heaven's Rejects. I clench my jaw, trying to push away the shame and embarrassment. I may have made mistakes in the past, but that doesn't mean Rigo is innocent. His son was a monster, and so is he. Gio just isn't here to answer for his crimes now.

The attorney continues, "In fact, we have provided evidence to show my client was not even in the state at the time of the alleged crime, evidence that the prosecution has refused to acknowledge or consider. Nor is this farce of a trial purely and simply a case of our government's overreach of power against a successful, self-made businessman."

My blood boils as I listen to Rigo's attorney spout these lies. I want to scream out, to tell the jury what Rigo and his family did to me and countless others. To show them how much of a monster he is. I want to show them the scars his son left on my body.

But I know I can't do that.

I must trust in the justice system, the evidence, and the truth.

I glance at Callie, who's giving me an encouraging nod. I take a deep breath and try to focus on the task at hand.

When the defense attorney finishes, it's my lawyer's turn to speak. Callie stands up confidently, straightening her navy dress before casually moving toward the jury. "Ladies and gentlemen of the jury, you have heard the defendant's counsel try to discredit the evidence against Rigo Zezza. But let me remind you, the evidence presented in this case is more than enough to establish his client's guilt beyond a reasonable doubt."

She walks closer to the jury box, looking each of them in the eye. "Ginny Azzo has been a key witness in this case. She has provided testimony that put away dozens of his known associates, giving grieving families comfort in knowing the men responsible for the death of their loved ones are behind bars. And although the defense may try to discredit her, let me remind you she is not on trial here. Rigo Zezza is! And the evidence against him is overwhelming…"

She pauses for effect, letting her words sink in. "Rigo Zezza and his family have been involved in a long-standing criminal enterprise. They have committed theft, extortion, and even murder. They have destroyed the lives of innocent people, including Ginny. She is lucky to have escaped with her life. The same can't be said for the dozens of missing women last seen in his care. It is time for them to be held accountable for their crimes."

As Callie speaks, I can see the jury members nodding, their expressions shifting from confusion to understanding. They're starting to see through Rigo's lies and deceit, and I feel a weight lifting off my chest. Perhaps justice will be served after all. Callie moves back to our table, the confidence radiating off her.

"In closing, I urge you to consider all the evidence presented in this trial. To look past Rigo Zezza's façade and see him for what he truly is… a criminal who has caused untold amounts of pain and suffering. A man who deserves to be held accountable for his actions. The head of a crime syndicate who has terrorized this country for decades."

With that, Callie takes her seat, and the judge dismisses the jury for their deliberation. Each juror averts their eyes as they leave the jury box. None of them looking to Rigo or to myself.

"Let's get some air," Callie mentions, ushering me from my seat. My heart is pounding as we leave the courtroom, but I feel a glimmer of hope for the first time since this nightmare began. Maybe, just maybe, Rigo will be brought to justice. She hands me a paper cup full of water, but I never take a sip. My stomach churning far too much to even think about drinking it for fear it would come right back up.

The deliberation feels like it takes forever, my mind racing with all the possible outcomes. What if the jury still believes Rigo's lies? What if justice isn't served? I shake my head, trying to push those thoughts away. I must stay positive and have faith in the system. They can't let him walk from this, not when so much is stacked against him.

Finally, the doors to the courtroom open, and everyone scurries back to their seats. The tension in the air is palpable, and I feel like my heart is about to beat out of my chest. The judge takes his seat, and the jury foreman stands up.

"We, the jury, find the defendant, Rigo Zezza, guilty on all counts."

Relief floods through me, and tears sting my eyes. Callie squeezes my hand in excitement, and I hear clapping from the prosecution table. Rigo's cold gaze is now a thing of the past, replaced with a look of shock and disbelief. I savor the moment, feeling vindicated and validated.

The judge bangs his gavel and orders Rigo to be taken into custody until his sentencing hearing. I watch as the federal marshals escort him out of the courtroom, his expression blank. There's a sense of closure, like a weight has been lifted from my chest.

I'm free.

I'm finally free.

Chapter 3

SLIDER

PRESENT DAY

'I'M FREE,' Ginny writes in her latest letter.

It's over.

Ginny is free of the Zezza family once and for all.

A deep sigh rattles in my chest as the pent-up anxiety I had over her safety eases for the first time since I was imprisoned. I can only imagine what Ginny had to endure to finally break free. The thought is killing me from the inside that I couldn't be there with her every step of the way—to be her protector and comfort when she faced that rat bastard in the courtroom. I could only hope he'd end up here so I could enact my vendetta against the man who single-handedly ruined Ginny's life and stole so many years from her. Years I could have known her, and we could have been together instead of us both rotting away in our own prisons. Solace is now my only friend, knowing she's free. She is all that matters.

The rest of her letter details the court case. How she felt up on the stand in front of that fucking monster. Yet, there's not a word of what she's planning to do with her newly found freedom, leaving me to wonder where she is now, what she's doing, and who she's with. Ginny is one of the only people who ever cared about me and would do anything to protect me. But now she's free, I can't help but feel like a part of me is missing—the one good part of me still left.

Flipping to the envelope, I study the postmark. The date is five months prior. Her case had concluded many months before, and this is the first I've heard of it—a letter months after the fact. I'd seen Raze only a month ago, and he hadn't mentioned it. Did he not know? Had Ginny left the club and her brother in the dark?

If I know her brother as well as I think I did, I can't imagine he didn't have Voodoo keeping tabs on the situation. If motivated enough, he could find the proverbial needle in a bottomless swamp, which is why the Feds wanted his notorious hacker ass under lock and key. Ratchet would not be so careless with

Ginny, not after everything they'd been through together. So why did Raze not mention it?

I search the rest of her letter for clues but find none.

I can't help but feel a wave of anger. How long has Raze known? How long has her brother known she was free? Neither of them had given it a second thought that I should have been told immediately. Thus, denying me the peace of mind I desperately craved. But then, as I read her words again, I see the pain and sadness that lies beneath her simple declaration of freedom. I realize I've been selfish, too caught up in my own worries, to truly appreciate what Ginny has been through. I've been so focused on getting her freedom that I hadn't considered the road she had to travel to get it.

I put down the letter and close my eyes, taking a deep breath to calm my nerves. It's been so long since I've felt anything but fear and desperation, and the sudden rush of emotions is overwhelming.

Ginny is free, but I'm still here, trapped in this miserable existence with nothing but my thoughts for company. I don't know how much longer I can take this shit.

I pace back and forth in my small cell, my mind racing with questions that have no answers. The only thing I do know is Ginny is free, and that's all that matters. But the nagging feeling in the back of my mind tells me things aren't that simple. And for someone like me, things are never simple. I need to know the truth. And I need to see, talk, and hold her again. We may have left things uncertain, but I always intended to return to her when my sentence was up. Had she done the same?

I close my eyes and picture her face. I can almost feel her touch, her warmth, how she'd wrap her arms around me when her brother wasn't watching, and the smile she thought she hid when I'd bring her a gift or crack a joke. Fuck, I miss her so damn much. And now that she's free, I need to find her. I have to know she's okay.

I sit at the small table in my cell and grab a pen and a scrap of paper. I start writing a letter to her, telling her I'm still here, waiting for her. I don't know where the letter will go or if it will even reach her, but I have to try.

As I finish the letter, I hear footsteps coming down the hall. I quickly tuck the letter away and stand up from the table. The door to my cell creaks open, and I see one of the older guards standing there, a grim expression on his face. "You have a visitor," he says, his tone serious.

"What's going on?" I ask, trying to keep my voice

calm. "It's Tuesday. Visitors don't come until Thursdays."

"Get up, inmate," he says, stepping into the cell.

I stand, feeling a sense of dread wash over me.

Something is wrong.

I follow the guard down the hallway and into the visitation room, my heart pounding hard. He bypasses the main room, leading me to one of the private rooms further down the hallway where I usually meet the club's lawyer.

The guard throws open the door, motioning for me to sit. He takes the cuffs at his waist, slaps one of them around my wrist, and attaches the other to a metal loop embedded into the table in front of me.

"What the fuck is going on?" I demand, my voice a low, threatening growl. The cuff at my wrist is clanking as I jerk.

The guard tests my cuffs against the loop. With a satisfied nod, he steps back toward the door and exits.

The door closes with a slam, leaving me alone in the small, enclosed space. Sweat beads on my forehead as I try to calm my racing mind, but fear still lingers. This isn't a normal visit. Something's up, and I can feel it in my bones. I sit, waiting for what feels like hours, but it's probably only been a few minutes, while I fiddle with the cuffs on my wrist, trying to find some comfort in the familiar sound of metal against metal.

The door opens again, and this time, a man in a tailored black suit steps through the door with a manila envelope in his hand. The heels of his shoes click on the cement floor as he rounds the table and takes the seat adjacent to me.

"Lucas Sterling," the man in black smiles. "I've heard a lot about you."

"Wish I could say the same," I grind out.

"Do you mind if I call you Lucas, or do you prefer that little nickname from your club? Slider, is it?" My road name rolls off his tongue with a smirk crossing his lips. "I'll never understand why riding a motorcycle comes with such stupid nicknames. Let me guess. You got yours after wrecking your bike."

I scowl in response. "I got it sliding into your mother. How is she, by the way?"

The man in black chuckles, unfazed by my comment. "I see you haven't lost your sense of humor, even in a place like this. Good to know that four years in hell didn't break you. You'll need that strength." He leans back into the metal chair, his hands folding across his stomach.

"Who the fuck are you?"

"I think you know who I am and what organization I represent, Mr. Sterling."

My eyes narrow. "Enlighten me." He wants to challenge me. Let's see how he takes it being turned back on him.

"Homeland Security. You can call me Agent Smith."

My eyebrows raise before I can stop the shock from registering on my face. I'd have pegged him for FBI or even CIA, but Homeland Security? That's certainly a surprise. "What does Homeland Security need with me?"

"All business, I like that." He smiles. "But let's not rush getting to know each other. I looked into your record... squeaky clean for a guy in a biker gang. Though, when you come from money and the infamous Sterling Steel conglomerate, money does do wonders to make things disappear."

I flinch at the mention of my family's business. The one I had been set to inherit until I decided the life of suits and a stick up my ass wasn't for me. My parents have three other sons to choose from to step into my shoes, anyway. No reason to put family fortune into the hands of my father's fuckup, as he liked to call me. Other than meeting Ginny, walking away from my family had been the best fucking day of my life. It's been almost seven years, and they have not once tried to contact me.

"How'd an heir like you end up in a gang like the Heaven's Rejects?"

Talking to this piece of shit about my family or my club isn't happening. Settling back into my chair, I go silent.

"I get it, Mr. Sterling. I see a guy like me showing up out of the blue asking questions about my family and gang, I'd stay quiet too. Maybe small talk isn't your thing." He leans back into his chair. "So, let's get down to business, shall we? I'm here because I have a proposition for you. Something you could benefit from."

I narrow my eyes, distrustful of the man's intentions.

"Not interested." The man slides the envelope across the table toward me. I eye it warily.

"Open it," he says.

I reach for the envelope with my free hand, my mind racing with possibilities. Inside, I find a stack of photographs—grainy black and white images, one right after another. I flip through them, unsure of what I am looking at, until a clear photo appears in the pile. There in black and white is Raze. His cut is on full display with the burning decay of a building behind him.

"Tell me about the Manuel Cartel."

"Who?" The question takes me by surprise. It had been a long time since I'd heard that name.

"The cartel that your club massacred in Mexico seven years ago." He shuffles the photographs, selecting from the bottom of the pile and sliding it in front of me—an image of a woman's body, a bloody bullet wound seeping between her eyes.

"Surely, you recognize the wife of your club president."

I shove the picture away, feigning disgust. "I don't know what you're talking about."

"I'm sure you do, but I get it. Talking to a guy like me about your club is the last thing you want to do. Though, it would be in your best interests if you'd like to leave prison anytime soon.

"Fuck off, asshole."

"I thought you'd say that."

"I'm not a narc."

"Everyone has a price, Mr. Sterling. It's only a matter of finding yours," he surmises. He reaches into his pocket, pulling out his cell phone. He punches the screen with his fingers before sliding it in front of me next to the discarded envelope. An image appears on the screen of a woman with raven black hair sitting in a park. Her face is hidden away from the view of the camera lens, but I don't need to see it to know who it is.

It's Ginny. Fuck.

"Your girlfriend certainly seems to be enjoying her freedom." He smiles, turning the phone back toward him. "Pretty little thing. No wonder Gio Zezza took a liking to her."

The mention of Gio's name sends rage surging inside me. "Don't you dare talk about her like that," I growl, pulling against my restraints. "What do you want from me?"

The man in black leans forward, a sly grin playing across his face. "Information," he says simply. "We want to know what you know about your club's dealings in Mexico."

I shake my head. "I don't know anything," I say, a cold sweat breaking out on my forehead.

They had left me behind with V. The only thing I knew was that they had left and came back. The details weren't offered to me.

"You were in the inner circle. You must know something," he presses. "If you don't cooperate with us, we'll make sure your little girlfriend pays the price." He points to the phone with Ginny's image on it.

I feel a surge of fear and anger rise inside me. They wouldn't dare hurt her. She's innocent in all this. But still, I can't risk it. I have to protect her.

"Inner circle?" I laugh. "Dude, I'm just a damn

prospect. I wash bikes, serve beer, and do the bitch work. I am about as far as you can get from the *inner circle.*"

"For now," he smiles. "I think it's time you get a promotion, Mr. Sterling."

"That's not up to me." A prospect doesn't choose to become a patch. The club officers make that decision. If this motherfucker thinks I have a way to change the bottom rocker on my cut, he clearly knows nothing about MC life or how our brotherhood works. "If you think you can come in here and strong-arm me, asshole, you've got another thing coming."

"That's too bad." The man shoves up from his seat. "All I want is information, Mr. Sterling. Information that would help set you free and keep your pretty little plaything living a carefree life."

"You think you can use Ginny against me?"

"Smart man," the man in black nods. "I knew you weren't as stupid as that nickname of yours. We know your club was involved in the Manuel Cartel massacre seven years ago. What we don't know is why the club became involved and what else they have planned. And that's where you come in."

"You want *me* to give *you* information on my club," I say, feeling the weight of the situation settling heavily on my shoulders. "And if I refuse?"

"Well, we could always send Ginny to prison. I'm sure we can dig up something from her time with the Zezzas. I doubt her hands are as clean as she portrays them to be," he says, his tone almost cheerful. "Or we could try something a little more… persuasive."

"Fuck you." I snarl.

The man just smiles, a look of amusement on his face. "I knew you'd say that, which is why I have a little incentive for your cooperation." He unlocks his phone again. This time punching in a number, the sounds of the keypad echoing in the room.

"Do you have eyes on her?" he barks into the phone.

"Affirmative," the voice on the other end answers.

"Show me." His cell beeps before the sounds of a video call connect. He shows it to me, and there on the screen is Ginny talking with Ricca's little brother, Asher. Fuck, he's gotten so big. A black van pulls up behind Ginny and Asher. Neither of them noticing it in the crowded park. The door slides open, and I see a scope poking out of the open space.

My stomach drops. *Fuck.* "Touch a single hair on her head, and you'll regret it, asshole."

"Last chance, Mr. Sterling. Give me what I want, and I'll call him off."

"I can't give you what you fucking want, man."

"Suit yourself." The agent eyes me with a look of smug satisfaction. "Do it," he orders.

The words are like a punch to the gut, and all the breath leaves my lungs in a rush. *He's going to kill her.* Suddenly, every rational thought evaporates, and all I can think of is getting to her.

"Wait!" I shout, my eyes trained on the view in the man's phone. "Just wait. I'll do it."

The man smiles, eyes twinkling.

He hit the jackpot.

"Good. You've made the right decision, Mr. Sterling."

Chapter 4

GINNY

"ASHER, COME ON!" I bellow down the hallway of my brother's house. "You're going to be late for your soccer game."

Lord, I sound like a mom rather than the cool aunt I've decided I want to be. If a sixteen-year-old me could hear me, I'd be kicking my own ass.

"Asher, move your butt!"

"I'm coming." I hear him cry out as a thud comes from down the hall, and a muffled swear comes from the direction of his room. Though I can't make out what he's said, I hear enough syllables to figure out that my brother clearly hadn't been watching what he was saying around him.

His mop of curly dark hair bounces as he jogs to join me in the living room. He's grown up so much since the last time I saw him. The little boy I'd left behind is fast growing into a teenager, something I don't think any of us are ready for just yet. Asher adjusts his bright yellow soccer jersey, scoffing when he notices a dark stain along the hemline. He scrubs at it with his hands. "Great," he huffs.

"Dude, since when do you care about a little dirt stain?" I remark, tousling his curls.

Asher glares back at me.

"What's her name?"

His head jerks up from his fixation on the stain, shock registering in his dark eyes. "I don't know what you're talking about," he retorts.

"It's Beth, isn't it?"

"No," he blurts out. "She's my friend."

"Who happens to be a girl and your best friend," I tease.

"And?"

"We picking her up on the way?"

"She has a ride," he mutters, stepping away from me to grab his soccer bag from the couch where my sister-in-law had placed it before she left this morning.

Try as he might, subtly isn't his strong suit. Beth and her family have been staples in our lives since I came back in December. After tragically losing their parents, the club rallied around the Bishops. Beth and her little brother, Carter, live with their older sister, Abigail, in one of the club's rentals and helped out with the security business Raze had been trying to get back off the ground. Carter, who'd been battling cancer at the time, had become the entire club's kid. We all worked out a schedule to make sure he had support for his treatments, doctor's appointments, and various other medical visits until his recent remission. While much more reserved than her other siblings, Beth is a mainstay here with us, always sticking close to Asher's side like a shadow.

I pull my keys from my pocket, spinning them around my finger. "Come on, Casanova. Let's get you to your game on time for once."

As we walk out to the car, Asher barely contains his excitement. I know he cares about soccer more than anything, but there's something else going on. I can see it in the way he stands taller and keeps checking his phone. I decide to let him have his secrets for now, but I'm definitely going to keep an eye on him.

We make it to the game just in time for Asher to join his team on the field. I find a spot on the bleachers and settle in to watch him play. He's always so focused when he's on the playing field, his fiery determination making up for his lack of size. Beth, who plays opposite him, kicks him the ball. He lights up at the successful pass and charges down the field. With a swift kick, the ball soars back to the opponent's goalie and slams into the net behind him.

"Way to go, Asher!" I scream over the crowd's noise. Pulling out my cell, I fire off a quick text to my brother and Ricca to let them know how the game is going. They respond immediately. I know it's killing them to miss one of his games, but Jude being busy with the club and Ricca helping out Abigail at the security firm, I knew updates would make them feel a little less bad about missing the game.

I'm pulled out of my thoughts by a voice next to me.

"Hey there," a deep voice rumbles. I turn to see a man sitting next to me, his broad shoulders taking up more than his fair share of the bench. He's older, probably in his late thirties or early forties, but still in great shape. He's wearing a leather cut with a patch that reads 'Reaper' on the breast pocket. I know what that means—he's a member of one of the local motorcycle clubs, just not the one my brother belongs to.

"Uh, hey," I say, unsure what to make of this situation. I've never interacted with someone from another MC.

"I'm Roman," he says, holding out a hand. I take it tentatively.

"Ginny," I say, my voice barely above a whisper.

"That your son out there?"

"Nephew."

"Ah." He smiles. "My daughter is number twelve on the other team."

"She's been hot on my nephew's heels all day."

"That she has… ruthless little thing. Takes after me." He smiles. A pregnant pause lingers between us. "First time at a game? I'd think I'd remember such a pretty face sitting in the stand with me."

"Not new," I fire back. "I'm normally here with my brother. He's a biker too."

Interest clearly piqued, he scoots closer. "That so? Which club? Maybe I know him."

"Heaven's Rejects. He's the enforcer for the club."

"You're Ratchet's sister?" he asks, his tone colder than before. "I didn't realize."

"It's not a problem, is it?" I ask, trying to keep the conversation light. My brother's club may have a beef with his for all I know, and stirring the pot between them is the last thing I want to bring to the club's doorstep after what they've done for me.

Roman shakes his head. "No, of course not. Just wasn't expecting to see a Reject here."

"I'm not a Reject."

Roman laughs. "Sugar, you may not wear a property patch, but they own you. Especially with Ratchet as your brother."

I can feel the tension between us, and I'm not sure how to diffuse it.

Thankfully, the game ends, and Asher jogs over to us, grinning from ear to ear.

"We won," he exclaims, leaning in for a sweaty hug.

"That's awesome," I say, patting him on the back.

"Hey, Ash, this is Roman. He's the dad of the girl who played opposite you today."

Asher looks up at Roman, sizing him up, his eyes narrowing.

"Good job today," Roman replies. "You're a hell of a player."

Ignoring Roman almost instantly, he switches his attention back to me. "Can we give Beth a ride home?"

"Sure, buddy. You go get your stuff and meet me back here."

Ash jogs back toward his team, leaving Roman and me alone once more.

"Sweet kid," he remarks.

"He is."

I allow the silence to fall between us once more. Roman's glance flitters between the phone in his hands and me. He turns just enough that the patch on his cut angles so I can read part of the top rocker.

'Twisted' is all I can make out.

He types away on his phone until Asher returns with Beth in tow.

"Ready to roll, guys?"

"Yup," Asher answers for both of them. Just as we're about to leave, Roman's daughter joins him. As we start for the parking lot, so do they. I watch him intently, noting his position and our surroundings. After dealing with dangerous men my entire life, I've learned never to take a situation at face value. At any moment, the tables can turn on you.

I can feel Roman's eyes on me again as we make our way to the car. "Nice meeting you," I say over my shoulder.

"You too," he replies. "Tell Ratchet I said hi."

I nod, getting into the car and shutting the door.

Asher is chatting away with Beth in the back seat, replaying every detail of the game, but all I can think about is Roman and the strange interaction we just had.

Something about him makes me uneasy, and I'm not sure I want to cross paths with the man again. I keep my eyes on the mirrors, watching for Roman or anyone else on a bike who could be following us to Beth's house. I circle a few times before dropping her off at her house just as Abigail pulls into the drive-way. They both wave goodbye as we back out.

As we drive home, I glance in the rearview mirror and catch Asher sneaking a few glances at his phone.

"What's going on with you?" I ask, trying to sound casual.

"Nothing, just checking some messages," he mumbles, avoiding my gaze.

"Anything you want to share?" I press.

He looks up, and I can see the excitement in his eyes. "Ratchet is coming home tonight," he says, his voice full of wonder.

I feel my heart drop at his words. My brother has been away on a run with the club for the past few days, and I thought he wouldn't be back for another week at least. Where the club is involved, you never know how long they'll be gone. It could be hours, days, or even weeks. Ratchet had warned me this run would be on the longer end and had asked me to help Ricca with Asher since he would be gone.

"What? When did he tell you that?" I ask, trying to keep my voice steady.

"He messaged me before the game," Asher grins. "Can we swing by Luca's to grab a pizza? I can order it."

"You know how to do that?" I feign surprise.

"Duh," he fires back. He pokes away at his phone while I reroute us back to the Luca's.

"Ordered. Said it would be ready in ten minutes."

"Just enough time for us to get there."

We pull up to Luca's, and I wait in the car as Asher runs inside to grab the pizza with the cash I'd given him to pay for it.

As I wait in the car, I can't shake the anxiety that has been creeping up on me since the game. The more I think about Roman, the more unsettled I feel. I know my brother's club has had its fair share of clashes with other clubs, and Roman's club might be one of them. But then again, I could be overthinking things.

Asher comes back with the pizza, grinning from ear to ear. "Can't wait to see Ratchet," he says, breaking me out of my thoughts.

I nod, still lost in my own head. "Yeah, me too."

The rest of the ride home is filled with Asher's chattering and the radio playing in the background. When we arrive home, I make sure Asher finishes his homework before allowing him to indulge in the pizza once Ricca makes it home. The excitement is palpable between us, and I can't wait for my brother to come home, either.

Asher heads off to bed shortly after ten, with Ricca doing the same not long after.

As the night wears on, I feel my anxiety spike again. My mind keeps going back to Roman, and I can't shake the feeling that something is off. I try distracting myself with television, but I can't focus.

It's past midnight when the sound of a motorcycle engine outside jolts me out of my restless thoughts. I rush to the door and open it, relief flooding me as I see my brother's bike parked outside.

Ratchet walks over, a tired smile reaches his eyes. "Hey," he says, pulling me in for a tight hug.

I hug him back, feeling my shoulders relax for the first time since the game today. "Hey," I reply, my voice muffled by his leather cut.

He pulls back, looking at me with concern. "What's wrong? You look like you've seen a ghost."

I shake my head, trying to push my fears aside. "Just had a weird encounter today with someone at Asher's game. His name is Roman and, I don't know, he gave me a bad feeling. His road name patch said Reaper."

Ratchet's expression turns serious. "What motorcycle club is he with? Did you see the back patch?"

I shrug, not sure. "All I could see on his rocker was 'Twisted.' "

Ratchet's eyes narrow. "Twisted?" he mutters,

shaking his head. "What else did you see? What colors were on his patch?"

"I'm not sure. I didn't see the logo."

"You're sure you saw 'Twisted?' "

I nod.

"Not possible. They're gone," he mumbles under his breath.

"Maybe I read it wrong." I shrug. "I barely got a look at it. I was trying not to be obvious." My heart sinks at his words. "Do you think he was here for Asher?"

Ratchet shakes his head. "I doubt it. We've done our best to keep Asher and Ricca out of club business. Probably just a guy looking to get laid."

"I'm not so sure. He knew who you were, Jude. He said I should tell you hello. He knew your road name."

My brother's face turns murderous once more. "That motherfucker said to tell me hi?"

I nod my response. "That's why it weirded me out so much. It's like he knew who I was before approaching me." The idea churns inside of my stomach. If Roman knew who I was, it wouldn't take much for him to put two and two together of who Asher is. The poor kid had been through enough with his abusive fuck of a late father and a drug-addicted prostitute mother. It pains me to even consider what his life would be like had Ricca not fought so hard to gain custody of him.

"I'll take care of it, Gin. I'm sure it was a one-off thing, but I'll text V to have him do a little recon. If this guy is local, he'll find him."

I nod, feeling slightly more reassured. If anyone can track someone down with minimal information, it is Voodoo. He'd found Ricca in Kentucky from her mother's obituary and a high school yearbook photograph. He's that good at what he does.

"How was your run?"

"Long. I'm glad to be home. Did Asher save me any pizza?"

"Nope, but I ordered a second one for delivery after he went to bed. It's in the oven waiting on you."

He wraps his arm around my shoulder as we head inside his house. "You're not half bad for a little sister."

While my brother disappears down the hall to change out of his road clothes, I pull out the pizza from the refrigerator, grabbing a couple of slices on a plate to warm up for him in the microwave. Jude returns a few minutes later wearing his pajama pants and an old band T-shirt.

"Smells good," he mutters, sliding into his seat at the kitchen table as I push the plate over to him. He finishes his pizza in record time.

"There's something we need to talk about, Ginny."

"About the guy from earlier?"

"No," my brother shakes his head. "Raze got a call earlier on our way back. Slider is getting out this week."

"He's coming home?" My voice is shrill and uneven, like the child I once was.

"He's coming home."

Chapter 5

SLIDER

HERE ARE YOUR PERSONAL BELONGINGS," the officer stationed on the other side of the glass mutters. She pulls out a paper sack, retrieves all the items inside it, and reads them off one by one in her manifest.

My clothes. My cut. My wallet. My dead-as-fuck cell phone. As she checks them off her list, she shoves them through the small opening at the bottom of the glass barrier toward me.

Gathering my belongings in my hands, I glance around.

"Bathroom's over there," she grumbles, pointing to a metal door to my left.

"Thanks."

I walk toward the metal door, struggling to keep my belongings together in my hands as I push it open. It's dimly lit inside, with a strong smell of bleach invading my nostrils. I wince as I step inside, closing the door behind me.

Taking a deep breath, I finally feel a sense of relief. The taste of freedom is on my lips for the first time—freedom that had come at a great cost, one that, even days after my last interaction with the nameless agent, still has my mind reeling. *Can I really betray my club for Ginny?*

I peel off the orange jumpsuit I've been forced to wear and throw it to the floor. The mirror on the wall reflects my tired eyes and rough stubble. I grab a paper towel and wet it under the sink, using it to clean my face.

My eyes wander toward a small window near the ceiling. It's barred up, but seeing the sky outside gives me a small glimmer of hope. Hope that the deal that got me out will not be my end, and I'll figure out a way around this to protect the club and Ginny at the same time.

Opening the bag, I retrieve my clothes. As I dress, I feel my mind racing with thoughts and doubts, along with the memories of Ginny's soft voice urging me to do the right thing. *But what is the right thing when all your choices lead you down a path of destruction?*

I take a deep breath, trying to push away the memories that keep creeping up in my mind. I need to focus on the here and now if I want to find a way out of this mess.

I glance at my cut lying on top of the bag, the club's emblem emblazoned on the back. It's a symbol of brotherhood, loyalty, and the life I've chosen. But now, it's more than that. It's a weight on my shoulders and a reminder of the choice I made.

I pick it up and put it on, feeling the leather hug my skin. It feels good to be back in it, and like I'm a part of something bigger than myself again. But at what cost? I know I had no choice. My loyalty to my club or Ginny's life? An impossible decision.

I reach into the bag to pull out my cell phone when my fingers graze something unfamiliar. Retrieving it, a box appears. Inside it is a second cell phone and charger with a note.

Keep this on you at all times.

My stomach drops.

It's real.

This whole fucking situation is real.

The heavy burden of the realization hits me like a ton of bricks. This is the cost—the cost to keep her safe, and I willingly accepted. Putting it into my cut reluctantly, I peer in the mirror again. The reflection is more like me than in the orange jumpsuit, but below the surface, the kid who walked into this place is well and truly gone. The man who's leaving is a stranger to me.

I take a deep breath and exit the bathroom, determined to find a way out of this mess, and make my way toward the door.

As I pull it open, the bright light of the hallway dazzles me, and I squint my eyes. The officer is standing there, her arms crossed, eying me suspiciously.

"Glad to be out?" she asks, indicating she doesn't really care.

I nod, hoping to get out of here as soon as possible.

"Well, this is the end of the line for you. Make sure you don't cross it again."

Believe me, lady, this is the last place I want to be.

"Ride's waiting outside."

I follow her through the gloomy hallway and out the door, greeted by the bright sunlight. The heat hits me like a slap in the face, but it's a welcome change from the prison's icy cold corridors. Stepping outside, I see a cab sitting at the curb, relief wafting through me that it's not one of my brothers here to get me. Prior to the deal, I would have been pissed if they didn't come for me, but the chance to figure out how I'll do this on the way back is a welcome relief.

I have a part to play and no idea how to do it.

"Safe travels." She smiles.

I nod my appreciation and step out of the building, breathing in the fresh air for the first time in what feels like an eternity.

The officer steps back inside the building, the loud clank of the heavy metal door striking behind her.

As I approach the car, I watch for any signs of trouble. The driver, a burly man with a buzz cut, is leaning against the car, smoking a cigarette. He nods as I approach and opens the back door for me to get in.

The leather seat feels soft against my skin, and I sink into it with a sigh of relief.

The driver gets in the car, and we start moving. "Where to?" he asks, his eyes fixed on the road ahead.

The clubhouse is the last place I want to be right now, not until I figure out this shit in my head.

"Red Rockets. It's a bar."

"I know the place," the driver replies, and the car speeds up, leaving the prison behind.

I lean my head back against the seat, my mind racing with thoughts. The box with the second cell phone weighs heavily in my pocket.

The streets fly by in a blur as the taxi makes its way to the bar. I can't help but feel like I'm on the brink of something big and dangerous. The deal that got me out of prison has put me in a precarious position with my club, and I know I have a lot to figure out if I will make it out alive.

As the cab pulls up to the bar, I pay the driver with the cash from my wallet and step onto the sidewalk. Red's bar has been fixed up a bit more since the last time I'd been with my club. It had been the dictionary definition of a dive, but now, the façade looks almost normal. The outside has been completely renovated—the ramshackle wooden exterior has been replaced with red brick. Even the landscaping has been redone at some point. I guess things really do change when you go to prison.

Walking to the door, I sigh before opening it. The bar is quiet, with only a few people scattered throughout the room. A couple of guys in polo shirts are sitting at the bar, nursing their drinks. A group of young women is sitting in a booth at the back, giggling and sipping on their cocktails. I take a deep breath and make my way to the bar, sitting next to the two guys.

The bartender steps to me. "What will you have?"

"Beer. Coldest you got."

He nods and pulls a bottle out of the refrigerator, popping the top off and sliding it toward me. As I take a long drink, I scan the room, looking for any signs of danger or trouble. The guys beside me are engrossed in their conversation, not paying attention to me. The women in the booth are giggling even louder now, oblivious to their surroundings. But I know better. In this life, you can never let your guard down, even in a seemingly harmless place like this. By the third swig, it's empty. I wave my empty bottle at the bartender who quickly slides over another one.

I already feel the weight of my choice pressing down on me again. The second cell phone in my pocket is a constant reminder of what's at stake. I know I have to be careful and play my cards right to protect Ginny and the club. But what if I'm not strong or smart enough to pull it off? What if my loyalty to Ginny and the club proves to be my downfall? The thought chills me to the bone, and I take another long drink of my beer, trying to drown out the doubts and fears in my head.

But as I set the bottle on the counter, I know I can't run from the truth forever.

"Mind if I join you?" a voice says from my left.

I turn my head to a woman with blonde hair cascading down her shoulders, smiling at me. She's wearing a tight red dress that hugs her curves, and her bright blue eyes are fixed on me.

"Sure," I say, gesturing to the empty seat next to me.

She takes a seat and orders a drink, her smile never leaving her face.

"So, what brings a rough and tumble guy like you to a place like this?" she asks, her gaze fixed on me.

"Just getting out of prison," I reply, taking another swig of my beer.

"Ooh, bad boy. I like it," she says, her hand resting on my arm.

I can tell where this is going, and it's not what I'm looking for. The old me would have bought her a few more drinks and fucked her against the back of the building until I had my fill. Though Ginny and I had never gotten that far, and with my extended dry spell from prison, even the temptation of this pretty girl isn't enough to sway my resolve.

"I appreciate the offer, but I'm not interested," I say, pulling away from her touch.

Her smile falters, and she looks disappointed. "Suit yourself," she mutters, downing her drink and getting up from the bar.

The bartender brings me my third round as heavy footsteps approach me.

"First day out of prison, and this is where you come."

I spin on the barstool, drawing my beer up to my lips. Raze, my club president, stands behind me. His salt-and-pepper beard more salt now.

"Needed a drink." I shrug.

Raze slides onto the stool next to me, ordering a beer from the bartender. He takes a long swig before turning to me. "You know what you need more than a drink? Your club. The ladies have been planning for weeks for your homecoming party. Darcy will be hurt you stopped somewhere else first, but we'll keep that between us."

"How did you know I was here?"

"Red called me."

I peer up, spying Red watching us from the hallway where his office lies. He tips his head at me before disappearing.

"I wasn't aware I needed a babysitter," I growled.

"You don't."

"So why are you here then?"

There's a moment of silence between us, the sound of glasses clinking and chatter filling the air.

"Thought you might like to talk a bit before the rest of the guys and ladies mob you."

"I'm fine," I declare, taking another sip of my beer.

"You went to prison for four years, Slider. You aren't fine."

"I said... *I'm fine*," I repeat, my voice growing stronger. I don't want to talk about my time in prison. It only reminds me more of why I am out, why I will have to betray the man in front of me, and how I'll implode his life and the lives of all my brothers for Ginny.

"Look, I get it. It's your first day out. I don't expect you to be who you used to be, but our brothers want to see you. Especially V. He's been waiting a long fucking time to thank you."

"He doesn't need to thank me." None of them do.

"Yes, he does. He may have saved our ass, but you stepped up for him. Giving up part of your life to someone else isn't something just anyone would do. You did good, brother," Raze finally says, clapping me on the back. "We're all proud of you."

Guilt eats away at me. He shouldn't be. I'm going to be their undoing, and he's patting me on the back for it. My stomach lurches at the thought.

"Look, I get that you don't want to talk about it, but you can't keep everything bottled up inside. It's not healthy," he says, his tone softening.

My mind is still a mess, and I don't want to risk saying something that could jeopardize everything.

"I'm just trying to figure things out," I say, my voice quieter now.

"I know. And we're all here to help you do that. You're part of this club, Slider. We take care of our own," Raze says, clapping a hand on my back before getting up from his seat. "We'll talk more later. You need to save some energy for tonight."

"What's going on tonight?"

"Your welcome home party." Raze reaches into his pocket, pulling out his wallet and fingering a couple of twenties before sliding them onto the bar top. "Let's get you home. Your bike's outside waiting on you."

A home I am not sure is my home anymore.

Chapter 6

GINNY

MY EXCITEMENT and nerves are off the charts as I try to help Darcy, Presley, and Dani with the food we've been making all afternoon since Raze got the call from the club lawyers that Slider's been released. I'd begged my brother to let me be the one to get him, but my request was denied.

"You ready for this?" Presley mutters while we're slicing tomatoes for the burgers V is flipping on the grill outside.

"Are you asking as my friend or my therapist?" I fire back with a smile.

"Bit of both." She shrugs.

"I am." Those two little words are nowhere close to explaining the churning excitement of being able to see him again.

"Four years in prison is a long time," she reminds me.

"I know, I know."

Presley stops her slicing to turn to me, concern dotting her face. "He may not be the same guy who left, Ginny. I need you to understand that."

While her concern is noted, Presley and the rest of them have no idea what it is like to be locked away. Slider and I do. If I could make it out the same as I went in, so can he.

I nod to Presley, appreciating her concern. But as much as I know Slider may not be the same guy who left, I need to see him anyway. My mind is made up. "I need to see him, Presley," I tell her softly. "I need to know for myself."

"I understand," she says, sighing. "Just be careful. You don't know what he's been through."

I nod, knowing she's right. It's been four long years, and I'm sure Slider has had to endure things I can't even imagine. But I need him, and I know he needs me too.

As we finish up with the toppings for the burgers, I feel my heart racing in anticipation. I haven't seen Slider in so long, and I know it will be emotional. I'd only received his letters a few months ago. Four years of writing to me, and I had no idea. The man penning those words is the same as I remember him

—always trying to make light of his situation and full of concern for me.

V comes in from the back and hands me a plate with the burgers, and I take it gratefully, placing it on the buffet table the guys set up.

After we finish setting up the food, we head outside to wait for Slider's arrival. The sun is setting, casting a warm orange glow over everything. I take a deep breath, feeling the cool breeze on my face. It's finally happening.

Minutes later, we hear a motorcycle coming down the road, and my heart skips a beat. *This is it.* A moment later, Slider pulls up in front of the clubhouse, his bike purring softly. He looks different than I remember, but it's still him—the same rugged features and intense eyes that felt like he could see into my very soul. He takes off his helmet. His dirty-blond hair is much longer than I remember. He'd always had this California surfer thing going on for him, but now, it's something much more than that. Something I can't quite put my finger on. I can see the emotions playing out on his face—relief, happiness, and maybe a little anxiety.

My feet move on their own accord as I walk toward him. The rest of the group hangs back, giving us space. I hear my heart pounding as I finally stand before him, a million thoughts and emotions rushing through me all at once.

"Hey," I say, my voice barely above a whisper.

"Ginny," he says, his voice husky and filled with so much emotion it's almost too much for me to handle.

Without hesitation, he pulls me into an embrace, crushing me to his chest. I inhale his scent, feeling like I've finally come home. I wrap my arms around him, holding him tight. It feels like we stand like that for hours until we finally pull away from each other.

We're both smiling, but I see the raw emotions in his eyes. I know he's been through a lot, and I can only imagine what he's feeling right now.

"I can't believe you're finally out," I say, breaking the silence between us.

"Neither can I," he admits, running a hand through his hair. "It doesn't feel real yet." He nuzzles his nose into my neck, inhaling me like a drug. "Fuck, I've missed you."

"I've missed you." Pushing up on my tiptoes, I press my lips against his. He stiffens at first before relaxing against me.

My brother clears his throat behind us, drawing our attention away from each other and back to the crowd behind us.

"I take it he knows?" Slider asks me with a smile on his face.

"He figured it out." I shrug. Worry crosses his face, and I kiss him again. "Don't worry about my brother. I'll take care of him."

"Ginny, baby, I am always going to worry about your brother. I've seen the shit he's done." I'd watched him cut the balls off one of our enemies and feed them to him like it was a fucking cookie. Ratchet is the club's enforcer for a reason, a damn good reason, and crossing him is the last thing I want to do, considering everything else I'm facing.

I nod, understanding what he means. "Jude is just a big old teddy bear."

"You mean a living, breathing Chucky doll who is currently staring a fucking hole through me for kissing you."

I peer over my shoulder and spot Jude in the crowd behind us, fuming. "It'll be fine."

"You keep saying that like I should believe you."

"Come on," I say, taking his hand. "Your club is waiting for you."

As we walk toward the clubhouse, I feel Slider's hand in mine, warm and solid. I know we have a lot of catching up to do, but for now, it's enough that he's here.

The guys swarm him. Handshakes and manly

shoulder pats abound. Raze and the guys lead him inside. He glances my way over his shoulder before they push through the doorway.

"They are as bad as we are," Ricca remarks with a smile. "Bunch of overgrown, bearded mother hens."

The other ladies snicker at the thought.

"Is Jude okay?" I ask once Darcy, Dani, and Presley head inside, leaving me alone with my sister-in-law. "If looks could kill…"

Presley reaches out, taking my hand into hers. "I think he did rather well, considering he just watched his sister make out in front of the entire club."

"Slider thinks he's going to castrate him," I joke.

"The night is still young." Ricca laughs, linking her arm though mine as she leads me back into the clubhouse. "Though, I made him leave his go bag at home. Just in case." She winks.

As we walk through the crowded room, everyone is lined up at the buffet, Slider at the head with a plate in his hand. He heaps on food like a starving man before walking over to one of the tables. He drops his plate and then moves over to me.

"I'll fix you a plate," he declares before cutting back in line in front of the guys who protest. Once he's picked out a few things for me, he returns, holding out his hand for me to take, and leads me to the table he picked out.

Hero, Ratchet, and Thor join us. The four of them rattling on about club stuff while I focus on my meal.

I know they're all curious about Slider's return, and I can see the mixed emotions on their faces as they talk. Most of them are happy to see him, but a few look wary. I can't blame them. Slider has been gone a long time, and things have changed since he left. I can feel the tension radiating off him, and I know he's not completely comfortable yet. I reach out, taking his hand in mine.

"It's going to be okay," I whisper. "We'll figure it out together."

Slider gives me a small smile, squeezing my hand. "I know."

After dinner, the guys make their way toward the back of the room, where the bar is located while the ladies and our new prospect, Riddle, help clean up the mess. I watch as Slider orders a beer and sits with the guys on one of the couches.

Taking the last of the plates into the kitchen, a strong hand grabs me. I yelp as I'm pulled against a hard chest. Slider's clean scent fills my nostrils—the mixture of leather, sandalwood, and salty spray of the ocean that I missed so much about him.

"Come with me."

"But I'm not done helping clean up," I protest before his mouth descends on mine.

The kiss is like a bolt of lightning shooting through me and setting everything on fire. I lose myself in his embrace, feeling his arms tighten around me and his tongue seeking entrance into my mouth. I let him in eagerly, surrendering myself to the heat and passion that's been building between us for years.

We break apart for air, gasping for oxygen. "Fuck the dishes," he whispers huskily in my ear, his lips tracing a line down my neck. "Let me show you what I've been dreaming of all these years."

Chapter 7

SLIDER

THE MOMENT I laid eyes on Ginny again, the only thing on my mind was getting her alone and away from her brother's watchful eye. I would have done this much sooner had there not been an audience upon my arrival.

"Where are we going?" Ginny asks as she trails behind me.

"My room." I pause. "It's still there, right?"

"It is. I sleep in there sometimes." My heart swells at the thought that my room was her sanctuary in my absence, a sanctuary I plan on making into the altar where I worship every inch of her. I kick the door open, dragging her inside behind me.

She squeals when I spin her around, pressing her front into my chest. I walk us back, the door slamming shut behind us as I press her into it. Before she can let out a gasp, my mouth captures it, my hands gripping her hips tightly as I press myself against her. I've been waiting for this moment for so long I can barely contain myself. The kiss outside only stoked the fire inside me. I need more. My tongue forces its way past her lips, and we taste each other hungrily.

I can feel her heart racing against my chest as I kiss her deeply. My hands trail down her body, feeling every curve and dip. I can't get enough of her. It's been too long since I've had her this close. We may never have crossed this line before I left, but after tonight, that changes.

Tonight, I claim what's mine.

Four years of starving for her has a way to make even the most chaste man want to defile the sweetest of creatures. I intend on ruining her. I need more of her. I need to feel her wrapped around my fucking cock. I want to feel her fall apart as I fuck her, my cum dripping from between her thighs as I stake my goddamn claim.

Ginny moans against my lips, her hands gripping my shoulders tightly. I can feel her desire building, and I know she wants this just as much as I do.

I break the kiss, trailing my lips down her neck to her collarbone. I taste the saltiness as I suck on the sensitive skin there, leaving a mark. I want everyone to know she's mine.

With a swift movement, I lift Ginny, and she wraps her legs around me. I feel her warmth against me, and it drives me crazy.

"Fuck, Ginny," I growl. "You have no idea how good you feel. I'm like a man dying of thirst, and you're my only source of fucking water."

I walk us over to the bed.

"Finally, I have you in my bed, all to myself," I whisper, placing her dainty body down on the softness of the mattress. "Tell me what you want, Gin. Tell me how you want me to fuck you."

"Just fuck me. Please… I need you." Ginny looks up at me with bright eyes, her body flushed and wanting. "Please," she whispers. Her hands fall to her top, but I stop her.

"I've been waiting for this for far too long, baby. I'm not rushing."

"But…" she protests.

"No buts," I whisper, gently kissing her lips before standing up and taking off my shirt. I watch her eyes widen in anticipation and see the heat and desire pooling in her gaze.

"Not fair."

Leaning forward, I hover my body over her, my

arms falling to either side of her head. "Nothing's fair, baby, when it comes to how I want to love you."

I want to remember every moment of desire and pleasure that passes between us. With the threat of my deal lingering over me, moments like this may be all I have left in the end—moments I won't waste.

"Please," she begs again. The sound of her breathy voice is enough to make me reconsider taking this slowly.

"Take off your shirt," I demand. Ginny's hands fall to the hemline, jerking it over her head in one swift movement, the black lace bra she's wearing underneath on full display.

"Please tell me your panties match," I growl.

She coyly smiles up at me. "Guess you'll have to find out."

My mouth descends over her lace-covered breasts, biting her nipples through the soft fabric, the pebbled nubs peaking against my tongue. Ginny squirms underneath, her pelvis pressing upward toward mine, seeking connection.

"I need to feel you."

Pulling away from her, I lean up. My hips straddle hers, and my hands fall to the fly of her jeans. She hisses when I pry open the button.

"More," she pleads, undoing her bra.

My need takes over as I tug her jeans down, freeing her. My cock strains at the sight below me— Ginny's ample hips clothed in black lace. I'm beyond aching for her. My fingers slip into the warm dampness I find. My gaze is solely on her face as I slip further inside her perfect little cunt.

Ginny's breathing is erratic, her thighs trembling against my hand as I move my fingers, finding her sweet spot. I move my lips down her body, pressing open-mouthed kisses until I'm between her legs.

My mouth descends over her panties, shoving the sheer fabric to the side before finally tasting the sweet nectar that lies beneath—the perfect mixture of sin and sweetness. I'd been dreaming of devouring her like this for years. Those dreams and wants are nothing compared to the real thing. I'll never get enough of her.

Ginny's back arches up off the bed, grasping handfuls of the blankets in a tight grip. Her moans mingle in the air as I feast on every inch of her. Her hips buck against my mouth, and I surge forward. Ginny wraps her legs around my shoulders, her hands clawing at my back.

"Fuck." She hisses as I take her swollen clit between my teeth, pressing gentle bites between sucks and licks.

My motions become more desperate. I need to be inside her.

Pulling my mouth away, I take one side of the lace, ripping it in half. I do the same to the other side, pulling the remnants away from her body and laying her bare in front of me. She's perfect in every way, and I intend to show her just how much I appreciate her.

Tonight, I'm making up for every single second I've been gone.

I force myself away from her. I shove my jeans down my hips and off my legs before returning to the bed, Ginny's gaze never leaving mine. I reach over to my bedside table to grab a condom when it hits me. My stash is four years old. It has to be expired. "Shit," I curse under my breath.

"What?" she asks, leaning up on her elbows.

"My condoms are all expired."

Ginny smirks up at me. "I'm on the shot."

"The what?"

"It's birth control. I'm covered and clean."

The thought of taking her bare is almost too much. "You sure? Tell me this is what you want because once we cross this line, baby girl, there is no turning back. Once you're mine, I'm never letting you go."

Ginny doesn't hesitate, not even a second, before she answers me, "I'm yours."

Without hesitation, I shift and sink into her body, and a quiet moan escapes her lips as she welcomes me.

"Fuck." I hiss through clenched teeth as Ginny's body wraps around my cock like a vice. "You're so goddamn tight. It feels like your pussy is choking my cock." She squirms when I inch farther inside her.

"You okay?" I ask with a pause, my gaze searching her face for discomfort. "I don't want to hurt you."

"I'm fine," she reassures me. "It's been awhile." She pauses, unsure of what to say.

Me too, baby girl. Me fucking too.

"You sure?"

"Yes," she answers. "I've waited too goddamn long for this to let a little pain get in the way."

I push in a little farther, allowing her more time to adjust to my girth. I'm not exactly what you would call average in the dick department. I should have known to take it slowly, but having her here, naked and wanting, had clearly knocked the common sense clean out of me.

I search her face again, this time finding a frown. "Stop treating me like a porcelain doll, Slider. I'm not going to break."

"Yes, ma'am," I tease before pushing myself all the way in. Her back arches off the bed, which only drives her hips harder into me, shoving me more.

"Shit." She recoils. I am still inside her, allowing her the time she needs. I pull out slowly before pushing back inside her this time. She hisses again. I pull out again before slowly sinking myself back inside her. This time, Ginny doesn't buck away. Her body relaxes, and she melts around me.

"Talk to me, baby. Tell me what you need."

"More," she muttered against my neck, her teeth sinking into the flesh.

I smirk against her, driving in one solid thrust before repeating the motion over and over. Our bodies quickly grow slick with sweat as we move together.

Ginny wraps her arms around my neck, bringing my face to hers. Our lips clash as her muscles clench around me, threatening to pull me over the edge.

My strokes become deeper as my motions become more frantic. I can feel her body tense beneath me, her sweet moans filling the air around us.

I thrust inside Ginny harder and faster, pleasure and desperation coursing through my veins. I'm losing control and can feel her body quivering beneath me, responding to my motions perfectly like two pieces of a puzzle.

Ginny wraps her legs around my waist as I drive deeper into her. There is nothing but pleasure in this moment—an unbreakable connection being forged between us. Everything else fades as we become lost in each other. The world stacked against us no longer exists. It's just us here. Together, at last, where we were always meant to be in the first place. This is what I have been missing. *Ginny.* And with her, I can finally be free.

Her moans and cries fill the room as we go higher and higher, her pleasure tearing through me like lightning. My orgasm builds deep inside me as I move faster until I can't take it any longer. With one final thrust, I let go, spilling myself inside her.

My body collapses against hers, sweat drenching us both.

"I love you, Ginny," I whisper, my lips still pressed against her neck.

"I love you too," she cries, tears escaping her eyes.

Hearing those words from her lips seems surreal —a daydream I don't want to wake up from. We may not have had much time together before shit went south for us, but time is all we have now.

"You're mine," I tell her, holding her tightly.

"I'm yours." She nods, snuggling deeper into my embrace. "Always yours."

We may have been apart for four years, but I'm never letting her go again.

I have made a deal with the devil to keep her, and there's no turning back now.

Chapter 8

GINNY

IT HAS BEEN two days since our reunion. Two days spent in his bed, enjoying each other and sleeping in each other's arms—our attempt to make up for the last four years apart. Truthfully, sleeping and fucking, we've barely eaten a thing. He'd slipped out a few times to the kitchen only to return with a plate of leftovers or something simple.

I'd attempted to sneak out earlier this morning after waking up to a rumbling stomach, but before I could even get dressed, Slider had woken up and thoroughly convinced me I needed to get back into bed. I must have fallen asleep afterward because the sound of the door creaking open wakes me completely.

Slider steps into his room with two plates in his hands, a heavenly smell wafting off them. I sit up in his bed, craning my neck to see what he brought us. He settles one of the plates onto the bedside table while still balancing the other one and two drinks. A small stack of steaming pancakes loaded with butter and syrup sit in the middle of each plate, and my mouth nearly waters at the sight.

"You have to let me leave your room at some point in time, you know that, right? My brother is going to send out a search party soon if you don't."

Slider cocks his eyebrow at me. "He knows where you are."

"That so?" I tease him, retrieving the plate from the table while he settles onto his side of the bed. "Did you happen to see him this morning?"

He shakes his head. "No, but I know he'll be looking for you sooner or later. I have been defiling his sister for the past two days. We both know he's not going to let that shit go. Figure I should make sure you're fed before you decide to escape again, or he breaks down the door."

"Jude is many things, but he doesn't have a say in my love life."

Slider chokes back a snort. "Ginny, I think we both know that's a lie."

Rolling my eyes at him, I return my focus to my breakfast. I take a bite of the pancakes, groaning at the deliciousness of it. "Who made these?"

"I did." He grins, picking up his plate and fork.

I shovel two more bites into my mouth. The taste is even better than the first bite. "You made these? Where did you learn how to cook, and why haven't you cooked for me before?"

Slider smiles. "Had I been given the chance, I would have, baby. We didn't have a lot of time before. I need to make up for what we lost."

The reminder of those dark days before the world went to shit around us pulls me out of the happy little bubble we've built since he came back. We'd barely realized our feelings for each other before our circumstances ripped us apart. We may never get that time back, but he's right. We're together now, and that's all that matters.

"Where did you go just now?" he asks quietly.

"No place good," I admit. Shaking the uneasy feeling away, I smile back at him.

"Well, we're here now." He smiles, closing the gap between us with a kiss. "No more dwelling on the past... we don't need it. I have exactly what I want."

His eyes linger on me a moment too long, and my cheeks heat with a blush.

"Even if that woman is the most stubborn person on Earth, with a murderous brother who's apparently been blowing up my cell phone for the last two days?" I grab my phone charging on the side table and show him the string of texts from Jude, Ricca, and even Asher.

My laughter fills the room as he takes a bite of the pancakes. "Oh yeah. Even then."

We silently dig into our breakfast, lost in our thoughts. Every now and then, one of us will pipe up with a comment or joke about something.

Eventually, the food runs out, and Slider stretches, breaking us out of our food coma trance.

"So, what do you want to do today? We can stay in bed and see what trouble we can get into..." he suggests, leaning back against the pillows. "Or... we can rejoin society."

I smile, thinking about the possibilities that lay ahead of us. "I think we need to at least go see my brother and reassure him I am alive and not kidnapped, as his last text suggests." Slider leans over, planting a kiss on my cheek before taking the plate from my hand.

"Why don't you go get the shower started? I'll take these into the kitchen and be back to join you."

"I can take my own plate to the kitchen," I protest as I try to take it back from him.

He shakes his head with a laugh. "The last thing I need is for you to walk out into the clubhouse reeking of sex. I didn't see your brother out there, but the second you step out of that room like that, he'll be sure to show up. I'm not taking that chance. I like my balls right where they are." He leans over, kissing me on the cheek. "Be right back." Slider grabs his plate and disappears through the door.

I nod, feeling a mix of contentment and excitement. After all the chaos and uncertainty these past few years, relaxing and enjoying the company of someone I care about feels like a luxury.

As I make my way to the tiny en suite bathroom, I can't help but feel a twinge of nervousness. It wasn't just the thought of facing my brother or figuring out what to do next that had me on edge. It was also the fact that this was the first real relationship I had been in since everything had gone to hell. We may not have written an official declaration about what we are to each other, but we honestly didn't need to. He loves me. While others may want a grand announcement or declaration of love, the moment we'd shared is all I need.

I reach into the shower, twisting the faucet to allow the water to warm while I strip out of one his T-shirts, adding it to his laundry hamper on the other side of the vanity.

Stepping into the shower, I let the thoughts drift away and focus on the sensation of the water cascading over my body with the warm steam rolling out of the spray of water. I close my eyes, savoring the feeling of relaxation. I get lost until a cool breeze comes from the shower curtain being moved aside as Slider steps into the shower with me, his eyes trained on mine.

"Mind if I join you?"

"This was your idea," I point out.

"Right." He grins. "Saving water, I think it was. I'm told sharing is good for the environment."

I roll my eyes at him. "Of course, it is."

"Here, let me show you." He takes my hand and pulls me under the water, his hands running down my body before he captures my lips in a passionate kiss. My stomach flips as I wrap my arms around his neck, feeling his strong body against mine. His muscles seem to have muscles now. His time in prison was clearly spent on keeping himself in shape.

"I think you've missed me." He smiles after breaking away from me, the water dripping down his face onto mine. He deepens the kiss, and I feel his hands on my back, pulling me closer. We break apart, gasping for air.

"Turn around," he whispers against my ear before releasing me. I step back, pivoting on my heels carefully with the water in the tub. His hands fall to my waist, pulling me against him, his growing erection hard against my ass. "Put your foot up on the side of the tub."

I do as instructed, feeling his hands run up my inner thighs, parting my legs a little wider and giving him more access. He slowly inches up higher until he finds my core. His fingers brush against my sensitive bud before slipping inside me. I gasp, my hands gripping the side of the shower walls for balance as he slides his fingers in and out of me. His other hand holds me steady, pushing against my body as his fingers dance inside me, his name slipping from my lips.

"Lucas," he growls. "That's the only name I want to hear on your lips when I'm buried inside you, baby."

"Lucas," I mutter, testing it out.

"Fuck… the way you say my name, baby. There's nothing like it."

His lips find their way to my neck, trailing expertly over my skin while he touches me. His hands then travel to my back, tracing the lines of my spine as my breaths become increasingly shallow. I can't think or move as his hands move faster, and my orgasm builds.

I'm just about to tip over the edge when he pulls away, leaving me panting and shaking with need.

His lips hover near my ear, his breath coming in short bursts.

"Hold onto the wall."

His large hands grip my hips, pulling me back to him. With one thrust, he's inside me. The pain is less than it was the first night. My ex had been big, but Slider is on an entirely different scale. It feels like he's trying to tear me into two halves. But after the last few days, my body is adjusting to him more easily.

"Fuck, Ginny." He hisses. "The way you feel around me is too fucking good, baby. I'm never going to get enough of your pussy."

He thrusts harder and faster, my hips rocking with each of his movements. His hands move down my legs, his fingertips gripping firmly as he slams into me.

"I could fuck you every minute of the day, and still want more."

"Harder," I request, needing to feel him deeper inside me. He complies. The sound of our bodies slamming together echoes off the four walls of his tiny bathroom.

Three bangs come from the other side of the wall, dragging my attention away from the moment.

"Ignore it," he orders.

With each thrust, the pleasure builds until I'm in

an agony of pleasure, clawing at his back as if trying to hold onto him.

"I'm close." He increases his pace, driving into me hard enough that my fingers begin to lose their grip on the wall.

"Shit. Shit. *Shit!*" I call out before I let out a long and loud scream and come undone, my walls gripping his length and milking him until I make him roar. I collapse against the wall, my legs shaking as my knees give out. Within seconds, he follows me over the edge.

Slider takes a few steps back, his breathing ragged as he looks at me, his eyes dark and smoldering with love and lust.

The banging happens again.

"Whose room is on the other side of this wall?" I ask, unsure if I want the answer.

"V's."

A warm blush falls over my cheeks. "So, the last two days... he's heard everything?"

"Probably." Slider shrugs.

I smack him hard in the arm. "Why didn't you tell me, asshole?"

"Because I don't give a shit if someone hears you or me. We're together, Ginny. Sex is a part of that equation. He should stay with his wife if he doesn't want to hear it."

"You're terrible."

"For you, baby. Only for you. Now, let's get out of here before we both drown."

We clean up for real this time. He finishes first and steps out of the shower to let me finish on my own. A few minutes later, I emerge with a fog of steam trailing out the door behind me.

Slider is sitting on the edge of the bed, his gaze focused on me. "You look beautiful," he comments, standing up and walking toward me.

I feel my cheeks heat at his words. It doesn't matter how many times he tells me, it always makes me feel the same. "Thank you," I whisper, leaning in to kiss him.

He deepens the kiss, and I feel his hands on my back, pulling me closer. We break apart, gasping for air. "I don't think we should leave this room," he murmurs, his lips brushing against mine.

I let out a laugh, pushing him away playfully. "We can't be in here forever," I remind him. "We need to face the real world at some point."

He sighs but nods. "Okay, fine. I'll let you get dressed." He walks over to his closet and pulls out a shirt and jeans. "I think my shirt might fit."

"It's fine. I stashed some of my clothes in your closet when you were gone." Walking over to it, I slide the door open to reveal a few hangers with shirts, jeans, and leggings I had brought with me. "I kind of moved myself into your room."

"I noticed." Slider grins.

"You don't mind?" Uncertainty pools in my stomach. With everything that happened with the Zezzas, his room had become my safe haven and a quiet solitude away from my hovering brother. No one bothered me in here, and I felt closer to Slider even if he wasn't here.

He stalks toward me, pulling me against him, wet towel and all. "What's mine is yours, Ginny," he states firmly. "I wouldn't have it any other way." He kisses me again softly before letting me go. "We should go," he says quietly.

I nod and dress in silence, twisting my hair in a wet, messy bun. My heart is full, and my mind is calmer than it has been in days.

I'd been into battle and back, and I'm still standing, alive and unscathed.

Chapter 9

SLIDER

WE BARELY MAKE it out of the hallway before someone is calling my name. I try to ignore them, opting to continue our path toward the door, but Hero is relentless.

"Prospect," he yells.

"Fuck," I mutter under my breath. The last thing I want to deal with right now is the club. I'd been purposely distancing myself from them and staying in my room with Ginny to avoid any interaction. If I have no idea what's going on with the club, I can't use it against them.

Ginny notices my unease. "What's wrong?"

"Nothing," I tell her before turning to face the music.

Hero shifts from his seat at the bar, stalking

toward us. "Nice to see you're both alive," he jokes. "I need a second of your time."

"Ginny and I were just on our way out."

Hero's expression turns serious. "It's important. Club business," he says, gesturing to the open door of the meeting room.

I glance at Ginny, who nods her head slightly. She knows how important the club is to me, even if I've been trying to distance myself from it.

"Fine," I say begrudgingly. "I'll be right back."

Ginny releases my hand.

Following Hero to the meeting room, he steps inside, ushering me in, where I find the rest of the club waiting for me. Ratchet glares at me the moment I spot him. The rest of the guys sit in their seats. Irons and Thrasher, now patched, are on the far end with Tyson, our treasurer, closer to the middle with the other club officers.

"Take a seat, prospect," Raze demands from his seat at the head of the table.

I hesitate before walking toward the empty seat beside Ratchet. I'd seen him do more with less distance. Considering he and I hadn't had a talk about Ginny's and my relationship yet, it is safer for me to keep my distance.

The rest of the guys are all staring at me, their

expressions varying from annoyed to suspicious. I try my best to keep my expression neutral, but I feel the sweat building up on my forehead. I have no idea what they want from me, but I know it can't be good.

"I'm fine where I am."

"Chicken shit," Ratchet mutters low enough that only I can hear him.

Raze clears his throat before leaning forward, his eyes scanning the room. "We need to talk," he begins, his voice low and serious.

I swallow hard, my mind racing to figure out what he's talking about. It's not like I've been doing anything I shouldn't be doing—I've been keeping my nose clean, doing what I'm told, and staying out of trouble. Up until Agent Smith's appearance, I'd done exactly as Raze and our lawyer had instructed me to do. Out of sight. Out of mind.

My heart sinks. There's no way they could know about Smith's visit, could they? The prison I'd been in was more a federal white-collar-crime prison, considering I'd taken the fall for hacking and not capital murder.

I try to keep a poker face, but am freaking out inside. I have been keeping secrets from the club, and if they found out about Agent Smith's visit, things could go south fast.

"You've been with us for how many years, prospect?" Hero chimes in.

"Six, if you count my four years in prison," I answer honestly.

"And in that six years, you've built quite a reputation," Raze says, his eyes narrowed. "You've been distant, avoiding us."

"I have?" I question. My voice wavering.

"I know coming back after four years away can be an adjustment. No one is faulting you for keeping your distance," Hero adds from his spot next to Voodoo. "We're concerned that you weren't fully honest with us after you got out."

"About what? It was prison."

"I think you know," Ratchet interjects, his voice cold and accusatory.

My stomach drops. *Fuck, they know.* Somehow, they know. I can feel the tension in the room as I struggle to come up with a response.

"I don't know what you're talking about. I've been doing everything you've asked of me."

"Except being honest with us," Tyson sneers.

Suddenly, my back is against the wall, my heart racing as I try to keep my composure. I know I'm in deep shit. If they've found out about Agent Smith's visit, there's no telling what they'll do to me.

"Is this about Ginny? Look, Ratchet, I wanted to tell you…"

Ratchet frowns. "Not the time to bring up my sister, prospect," he warns me. "You and I will be discussing *that* later."

There's a long moment of silence as the club members look at each other, a silent conversation passing between them. Finally, Raze speaks up.

"Why did you take V's place?"

"I'd like to know that myself," V adds, leaning forward in his seat. "I made the deal with the FBI. Not you."

I swallow hard, trying to organize my thoughts. It wasn't like I had planned to take V's place, but when the opportunity presented itself, I couldn't help myself. I needed to prove to the club that I was an asset, that they could trust me, and if I could protect V in the long run, so be it.

"I took his place because I wanted to help," I say, hoping my voice doesn't betray me. "The club relies on him and his skills. You needed him. You didn't need me."

The room remains silent, the tension thick enough to cut with a knife. My palms are sweating, and my heart is pounding. I can feel the club members' stares burning into me, their suspicion and anger palpable.

"Is that it?" Raze asks after a long pause.

I nod, too afraid to speak.

"Take off your cut."

"Wait, what?"

Ratchet rises from his seat. His hands grasp the lapel of my leather cut, stripping it from me.

I know what this means. They're stripping away my club membership, my protection, and my family. A wave of relief swells along with the dread. If I am not a club member, Smith has no leverage against Ginny. The deal will be null and void.

"This has been long overdue," Raze says simply, his voice cold.

"You're not a prospect anymore," Ratchet adds, tossing my cut on the table.

I stare down at my cut, unsure of everything. I blink, struggling to process what I've just heard. I stand there for a moment, staring at them in disbelief.

This isn't happening.

This can't be happening.

Raze rises from his seat, walks toward me at the other end of the table, and stops short in front of me. "You're one of us now."

He steps aside as Ratchet places the top and bottom rocker of a patched member on top of my cut.

My heart races as I try to make sense of the situation. This is not how I expected things to go. I was prepared for the worst, but not this. The relief I feel washes away to pure horror. My worst nightmare come true, just as Agent Smith wanted. I'm one of them now. They're playing into his hand and don't even know they are in the game.

"Welcome to the family," Raze says with a small smile.

I look around at the club members, who are all nodding in agreement.

"You're one of us now," Hero nods in confirmation.

"And with that comes responsibilities you may not be ready for."

"I understand," I tell them, feeling the weight of my new status settle on my shoulders.

"Good," Raze says, his voice holding a note of finality. "Because now that you're a patched member, there's nowhere to hide. Everything you do reflects on us, and we expect loyalty and dedication above all else. Our secrets are now yours to keep and protect. Entering into our brotherhood is for life. Once a Heaven's Rejects, always a Heaven's Rejects until the road rises to meet you."

"Thank you," I say, barely able to find my voice as I try to hide how I truly feel. The weight of the patch on my cut and the responsibility that comes with being a full member is massive. But at the same time, I feel like a fraud. I haven't been completely honest with the club, and now they're making me a fully patched member.

There's a moment of silence before Ratchet speaks up, "Now, let's get back to the business at hand," he says, his eyes pointedly avoiding mine. "New business?" Ratchet straightens in his seat. "A member from another MC approached Ginny a few days ago at Asher's soccer game. Guy gave her the creeps."

"The fuck?" I blurt out. My heart stops beating in my chest. She'd been approached and didn't think to tell me? Not one fucking word. Though considering we haven't had much chance to talk, I still would have thought she'd have mentioned it. Smith's threat is bad enough, but adding in a second makes protecting her even more difficult. The last thing I want to do is force her to hide. She's done enough of that in the last four years. I can't do that to her again. I won't.

"Do we know who it is?"

"Guy goes by Reaper. Told her his legal name is Roman."

"Club affiliation?" Hero asks.

Ratchet runs his hand through his hair. "That's the issue. Ginny said she didn't get a good look at his cut, but what she did see… fuck, it doesn't make any sense. She said the top rocker had 'Twisted' on it."

The room erupts.

" 'Twisted?' " V says, his tone laced with disbelief. "They've been dead for years."

"Maybe they're trying to make a comeback," Hero suggests.

"I burned that place to the fucking ground," Ratchet snarls. "No one walked away from it. Not after what they did to her." His fists clench in front of him. While I didn't know the full extent of what happened at that house, I did know that's the day Ricca came to the clubhouse looking as if she had gone through hell. Whatever happened there, those bastards deserved what Ratchet rained down on them.

"Maybe it's just one of their old members gone rogue," Raze adds.

"We need to find out who this guy is and his angle," Ratchet says firmly. "And we need to do it before he gets any closer to my family."

There's a tense moment of silence before V speaks up. "I'll make some calls. See if I can dig up any information on Reaper and this supposed Twisted MC."

"Good." Ratchet nods in agreement. "My wife is on alert, but I think we need to keep a couple of guys on Ricca and Asher. He approached in broad daylight. There's nothing to say he won't try again.

"I'll take Ginny," I demand. Ratchet glares at me.

The heat from his stare is boring into my chest like a fucking laser straight to the heart. He may not like that I am with her, but if she's in danger, I'll be the one who takes her watch.

"You sure?" Raze asks, turning to look at me.

I swallow hard, feeling a sense of responsibility wash over me. I may not have wanted to be a full member, but now that I am, I have to step up and prove my worth. "I'm on it," I say, my voice steady despite the fear churning in my gut. "She's my woman. Her safety falls to me."

"Good," Raze nods. "Let's get to work then."

With that, the meeting is adjourned, and the room clears out. I'm left standing there, staring at my new cut, feeling the weight of the responsibility that comes with being a full member of Heaven's Rejects. The sense of relief that had washed over me earlier is now gone.

Raze's expression darkens as he looks at me. "You'll need to find out who it was and why they were talking to her. We can't take any chances with her safety."

I nod, my mind already racing.

Smith had threatened once.

Now, a possible resurrection of a rival MC.

The cards are stacked against me, and I don't

know how I can survive working both sides to keep her safe.

This is where my destiny lies—for better or for worse.

Whatever happens, I can't let her get hurt.

Not now.

Not ever.

Chapter 10

GINNY

"WHAT DO you think they're talking about in there?" I ask Darcy when I find her in the common room of the clubhouse with Roxie, who sits on the floor playing with two dolls.

"Who knows with them? Could be nothing, or it could be the end of the world. That's how it seems to go around here."

As the old lady to the club president and a former vice president, Darcy is the most seasoned female in the club. She's been here for some of the darkest periods of the club's history with her late husband, Jagger, and even more with her second husband, Raze.

"How do you do it?" I ask honestly. "How do you sit back and let them shoulder it all?"

I glance at the door, wondering what secrets the

men inside are keeping from us. It's not uncommon for the club to keep things under wraps, especially if they could bring trouble to our doorstep.

Oblivious to the tension in the air, Roxie giggles as she makes the dolls kiss. Darcy's eyes soften as she watches the girl play.

"Because that's what it means to be an old lady to the men of this club, Ginny. It all may seem new to you, but you'll get the hang of it. I promise."

"I'm not even sure I am an old lady. It's not like he's asked me."

"Sweetheart, you don't spend two entire days in a row with one of these guys and walk out a free woman. Trust me. He'll stake his claim if he hasn't already."

I nod and look at Roxie, noticing how she's staring at me with a curious expression. "What do you think about all of this, Roxie?" I ask, trying to change the subject.

"I think it's boring." Roxie shrugs as she sets her dolls down. "I want to go ride on the bikes!"

Darcy chuckles and gives Roxie a fond smile. "Maybe when you're a bit older, honey. Those bikes are dangerous."

"I'm not afraid," Roxie insists. "Daddy lets me ride with him."

"That's because you don't know any better, and

Daddy takes you when I'm not around." Darcy sighs. "Against my wishes."

I shake my head. My mind is still stuck on being an old lady to one of the club members. It's a lot to take in.

As if reading my thoughts, Darcy places a comforting hand on my arm. "Don't worry, Ginny. You'll figure it out. And if it's not for you, then it's not for you. There's no shame in that."

I nod, taking in her words. Maybe she's right. Maybe I'll figure it out. Or maybe I'll realize it's not for me after all. Only time will tell.

"At least in the meantime, you two can enjoy spending time together."

My blush expands up my cheeks. "I feel like I need to apologize to V. I think he might have over-heard us this morning."

"Honey," Darcy laughs. "The entire clubhouse heard you."

I groan, mortified at the thought of everyone listening in on my intimate moments with Lucas. "By everyone, you don't mean my brother, do you?"

Darcy scrunches her nose and nods her head.

"Great. Just great. I don't know what's worse. The fact that V overheard us or that my brother did."

"I guess I don't have to worry about staking my claim anymore."

Darcy raises an eyebrow. "What do you mean?"

"I mean, everyone already knows we're sleeping together. What's the point of him staking his claim?"

Darcy chuckles and shakes her head. "Oh, sweetie. You have so much to learn."

"Now, I have to worry about that and my brother, who probably wants to kill him for defiling me, as he would put it. What else can go wrong?"

"That's not something we ask around here. It tends to invite trouble," Darcy admits. "Now, Ratchet will be more of an ass than usual, but they'll work it out. V had to do that with Raze."

"Didn't Raze deck V for sleeping with his sister?" We'd only been here a few weeks when I spotted V sporting one hell of a black eye. I'd tried to ask Presley about it, but she didn't crack.

"Yeah, but he kind of had it coming. If you knew where said act happened, you'd be more shocked he's still alive."

I try to mask my shock and amusement at Darcy's admission. It's hard to imagine the calm, collected woman before me approving of violence, but then again, I suppose it's all in a day's work for the club.

I chuckle, imagining the scene between V and Raze. "Well, I guess it's a good thing that my brother has had four years to come to terms with my relationship with Slider."

"That's a good thing, all right." Darcy grins. "Just don't let him push you around, Ginny. You're your own woman and deserve to be treated with respect."

I nod, feeling grateful for Darcy's advice. It's not often I find someone I can truly talk to, and I appreciate her wisdom. Presley had filled that hole for me for years in protective custody as my therapist, but she's been busy with her new practice and expecting a new baby with V. Outside of our weekly scheduled sessions that my brother encouraged me to keep, I've barely seen her. It seems to be a common theme amongst the ladies outside of Darcy.

With Dani and Hero's new little boy, she barely leaves the house—five kids under the age of six. How she does it? I don't know. Ricca has taken a part-time job with the club's side business. I'd offered to help out, but my brother insisted I stick around the clubhouse and his house to help out with Asher and the Bishops for the time being. I wanted to be useful to the club in any way I could, so I did what my brother asked until a new opportunity presented itself.

"We need to schedule a girls' night," Darcy admits. "It's been too long since us ladies had a chance to hang out without the guys hovering around."

"I'd like that."

"Me too. It's much easier to talk about all those

juicy details without them listening in and trying to correct us." She smiles with a nod toward the meeting room door.

Just then, the conference room door swings open, and out strides Lucas, a serious expression etched on his face. My heart quickens as I take in his tall form, broad shoulders, and muscular arms. Even when he's angry, he's sexy as hell.

"Ginny," he says, nodding his head in greeting as he strides over to us. "Darcy, Roxie."

"What's going on?" I ask, my concern mounting.

He starts to answer me before V joins us and stops him. "Someone got a few new accessories," V announces, wrapping his arm around Lucas.

"New accessories?"

"You're looking at the newest member of Heaven's Rejects, ladies."

Darcy lets out a low whistle. "Well, well. Congrats, Slider. Did you have to pass some kind of initiation?"

Lucas gives her a smirk. "You could say that." His tone is flat—too flat for someone who should be over the moon about finally getting his patch.

"I guess that means we need to plan another party." Darcy laughs. "If I had known marrying Raze would make the captain of the party-planning committee, I might have reconsidered his proposal."

"Like hell you would have," Raze bellows out when he overhears her.

"Let's hold off on the party."

V's head jerks so fast in Lucas' direction he has to have whiplash. "No party? Dude, it's the best part of getting your patch. The booze. The ladies," he says with a smile before he realizes his mistake. "Er, um… no ladies. We get nuns actually. Ugly ones."

"I'm sitting right here, asshat," I fire back at him. "You bring in strippers to his patch party, and I promise you, you'll see just how much I am like my brother."

Lucas gives me a protective look, his eyes softening at my defense.

"I don't think it's the right time. I just got out of prison. I need to let things settle a bit.

V bristles at his words. "What things? It's the perfect time to celebrate. Dude, if you had only been at mine. Fuck, there were these Japanese twins Jagger brought in for me. Smoking hot. Best day of my life."

"Enough, V," Lucas warns him.

"Does your wife know that she rates second to Japanese strippers?" I fire back.

"Um… about that."

"No party until he's ready or I tell your wife about the Japanese twins." I smile at him.

"Just when I think you're the nice Azzo, you flip the tables on me. Fine."

Slider hesitates for a moment, his jaw clenching before he finally speaks, "Drop it, V. No party."

"Fine… suit yourself," V concedes, throwing up his hands in exasperation. "But mark my words, Lucas. You're going to regret not celebrating your patch properly."

Darcy nods in understanding. "I get it. We'll just have to celebrate in a more low-key way. Hey, maybe I'll invite those nuns you mentioned. This place could use some power of prayer if you ask me."

Lucas' expression doesn't change as V storms off. The tension in the air is palpable, and I can feel my anxiety rising.

"Mind if I steal my wife?" Raze asks before whisking Darcy away toward his office.

"What's going on? You seem really tense."

He sighs, his rugged features softening as he looks at me. "It's just… a lot, Ginny. Getting my patch, getting out of prison… it's a lot to take in."

"I'm here for you," I say softly, going to him and wrapping my arms around his neck. "Anything you need, just ask."

He pulls me close, his muscled arms wrapping tightly around my waist. "I just need you," he murmurs, pressing his lips to mine.

The kiss is slow and passionate, and I lose myself in it completely.

"Let's get out of here."

"What about talking to my brother?"

"Later," he insists. "Right now, I want to take a beautiful woman for a ride on my bike."

Chapter 11

SLIDER

THE PACIFIC COAST Highway stretches out before us. The winding seaside gives us some of the best views in the state and the escape I need after getting my patch.

Before my deal with Agent Smith, I would have celebrated with Ginny and my brothers all night, reveling in my status change and being accepted into the family at long last.

But now? Fuck, it complicates things.

Being a prospect gave me my out with Smith, unable to deliver to him what he wanted. For a split second, I thought they were going to strip my prospect patch and kick me out. That act alone would have saved us all, but here I ride, their colors emblazoned on my back, with Ginny pressing tightly against the one thing I have wanted for years and the same thing that will be my undoing.

I am truly and utterly fucked.

As we cruise down the highway, I can feel Ginny's warm breath on my neck and sense her body shaking slightly with each turn. She has to be cold. The jacket I gave her to wear is barely warm enough for a cool fall night, not for a seaside ride on my Harley.

"Hungry?" I ask her over my shoulder. She nods her answer. "There's a place not far up the road. We'll pull off."

We turn onto a side road and follow it for a few minutes before coming upon a small diner with neon lights flashing in the window.

"This is it," I say over the wind's howl, pulling off the road and into the gravel parking lot. It is almost empty, but for a few cars scattered around. Likely the locals who come for coffee to solve the world's problems one cup of joe at a time.

The smells of cooking waft over the parking lot and tickle my nose. It's a pleasant mix of hamburgers, meat, eggs, and onions, fresh from the grill. I can almost taste the tang of the mustard and ketchup and smell the caffeine and tobacco absorbed into the diner's walls from the outside.

"I hope it tastes as good as it smells," Ginny admits.

"Trust me, it's good food. I've eaten here before."

As we dismount and walk toward the entrance, I can see Ginny's eyes widen with excitement at the prospect of a hot meal. I take her by the hand, leading her inside.

The diner welcomes us with a low murmur of patrons' voices, a jukebox playing somewhere, and the scent of fresh coffee. There are a few empty booths, and we pick one in the corner.

We sit across from each other, and I can't help but notice the way Ginny's eyes sparkle in the dim lighting. She's so damn beautiful, and I can't believe she's with me. How did I get so fucking lucky? I feel a pang of guilt in the pit of my stomach for what I've gotten her wrapped up in. Spending the day with my girl should be easy—a moment shared between us and a memory made—but shoving down the shit show surrounding me is impossible.

"What are you getting?" Ginny asks, her eyes scanning the menu as well.

"I'm thinking… cheeseburger with fries and a milkshake," I reply. "How about you?"

"The same sounds good to me," she says, smiling at me.

The waitress, a curvy woman in her mid-fifties,

approaches us with a friendly smile. "What can I get you two?" she asks, a notepad and pen in hand.

Ginny rattles off her order first, then I add mine.

"Coming right up," the waitress says with a nod before walking away.

As we wait for our food, I take the opportunity to study Ginny. She's changed so much since the first time I met her. This beautiful woman's always been tough, but now there's a fearlessness in her that's both intimidating and alluring. She faced hell and back with the Zezzas and lived to tell the tale. Not many people could claim the same.

"What are you thinking about?" Ginny asks, breaking me out of my thoughts.

"You," I say.

She raises an eyebrow. "Oh, really?"

"Your brother said something in our meeting today that I need to talk to you about. Why didn't you tell me about the guy at Asher's game?"

Ginny blanches. "I didn't think it was important," she says softly. "I didn't want to worry you for no reason. You hadn't come home yet."

"It's always important when it comes to your safety," I reply firmly.

"I know," she says, her voice barely above a whisper. "I just didn't want to cause any trouble. I wouldn't have said anything to my brother, but something felt off about him. He knew Ratchet's name."

I take her hand in mine, feeling the warmth spread between our palms. "If something would have happened to you, Ginny, what I would have done would make your brother's record blush. When it comes to you, I'll burn the world to see you safe."

She looks at me with tear-filled eyes. "You don't need to do that."

"Yes, I do. I protect who I love, and I fucking love you. You know that, right?"

"I do," she admits.

"Promise me that if something like that happens again, you call me or your brother immediately."

"It won't," she declares.

"You can't say that for sure. Promise me, baby. You won't put yourself in harm's way."

"I promise."

Our food arrives at the table, and we both dig in hungrily. The cheeseburgers are juicy and savory, the fries are crispy and salty, and the milkshakes are thick and creamy, the perfect combination of sweet and cold. We eat in comfortable silence, enjoying each other's company and the delicious meal.

As we finish, I can't help but feel a sense of dread settling in the pit of my stomach. I know once we leave the diner, reality will come crashing back down on us—the danger lurking around every corner, the uncertain future. But for now, in this moment, we are just two people enjoying a meal together. And I'll cherish that for as long as I can.

"Ready to head back?" I ask, breaking the silence.

Ginny nods, and we pay the bill before making our way back outside. We're almost back to the bike before Ginny swears.

"Shit. I didn't leave her a tip. I'll be right back." Ginny releases my hand, heading back inside the diner. I watch from the parking lot as she approaches our waitress.

My phone begins to vibrate in my pocket. I pull it out, only to notice it's not my personal phone ringing. Reaching back in, I pull out the phone that Agent Smith sent back with me. The black plastic vibrates in my hand.

I hesitate but punch in the code. Drawing it to my ear, I answer. "What do you want?" I ask, keeping my voice low so as not to alert anyone who might be listening.

"Just wanted to check in, see how you're doing, and remind you of our deal, of course," he replies casually as if we're discussing the damn weather.

"I'm working on it," I growl.

"Is that so?" Smith declares, a hint of amusement

in his voice. "Explain to me how a seaside date is *working on it*, Mr. Sterling."

Dammit. He knows my location and that Ginny is with me. I scan the area, searching for anything out of the ordinary. The sandy beach stretches out before us, with people walking along the shore and cars moving slowly along the streets. The wind whips up off the ocean, carrying a salty spray and sand in the air. If he's out there, there's not fucking way I can spot him. The slimy bastard knows what he's doing. Too well.

"I have to say you certainly have good taste in women. The pictures I have of her don't do her justice."

I grit my teeth at his words, trying to control the rising anger within me. "Leave her out of this. She has nothing to do with our deal."

"On the contrary," he says, his voice deadly serious. "She has everything to do with it. You know what you have to do, Mr. Sterling. If you don't deliver what I want, your girlfriend *will* suffer the consequences."

My heart starts racing at his words, and a cold sweat breaks out on my forehead. I know Smith is not one to make idle threats. This asshole has the power of Homeland Security and the government behind him.

"I'll get you what you want," I say through gritted teeth. "Just leave her alone."

"I'm glad to hear it," Smith replies. "I gave you a few days to settle back in. It's time you start providing me with intel. You have three days."

"Three days?"

"Three days," he repeats. "Bring me something useful, and you and your little girlfriend stay free." The line goes dead, and I'm left standing there, my hands shaking with anger and fear.

Three days to produce information I don't have and start lying to my brothers in the club. *How in the fuck am I going to do this?*

Ginny emerges from the diner, smiling brightly, oblivious to the danger we're both in.

"Let's get out of here," I say, trying to keep my voice steady and somewhat upbeat.

She nods, and we mount the bike, speeding off toward home.

But I know we're not safe.

There are eyes on us even now, and our time is running out.

Chapter 12

GINNY

AFTER PUTTING off my brother for as long as we could, he'd finally called in his demand—a family dinner—his way of exacting Lucas and me to the carpet about our relationship. While I had told him about it from the beginning, Jude took great offense that Lucas hadn't come to him first to ask his permission like we live in Victorian England, and he has to protect my virtue. I'd tried talking him out of this entire thing, but Jude vehemently insisted.

While pulling up to their house, anxiety wafts off Lucas in thick waves.

"It'll be okay," I try to reassure him as he helps me off his bike after he dismounts.

"You sure about that?" he fires back. Lucas looks at my brother's quaint home, then back at me again.

"Do you happen to know where he keeps his go bag?"

"Why would I know that? I don't even know what that is."

Lucas frowns. "It's a black bag about this big." He uses his hands to demonstrate the size. "Filled with everything you need to kill a man."

"No clue." I shrug, feigning ignorance to the bag I knew for a fact Jude keeps on the bottom left of his and Ricca's shared closet. He'd shown it to me when I moved into their house after Christmas in the off chance I might have needed a weapon. Why my brother thought I needed to know where a bag of, what I can only describe as torture-chamber toys are located is beyond me.

"It'll be fine." I smile, patting him on the shoulder.

"Jude is all bark and no bite. It's not like he's going to murder you in front of Asher."

"You don't know that. He'd probably use it as a teaching lesson on how to correctly filet a human being."

"Maybe," I shrug. "Only one way to find out."

Lucas' eyes widen at the statement, but I can tell my attempt at humor is not enough to ease his tension. Taking his hand in mine, I lead him toward the front door of my brother's home. Sounds of laughter come from inside, which only serves to make me more nervous. Jude's laughter has always been tinged with an edge of cruelty, and I can't help but wonder what kind of verbal punches he's been practicing for this evening.

"I guess I shouldn't be surprised, though. You are related to Jude, after all."

I can't help but smile at his reaction, feeling grateful to have him by my side as we make our way to the front door. He pauses, turning to me.

"We could say something came up?" His arms wrap around my waist, pulling me tightly against him.

I push him away playfully as my cheeks flush with embarrassment. "Focus, lover boy. We have a family dinner to get through. You're lucky Jude didn't pull open the door just now. He has this entire place wired with cameras. He's probably watching you right now."

Lucas grins widely, a mischievous glint in his eyes. "Does that mean I have to behave myself?"

I laugh and shake my head, taking his hand in mine as I knock on the door. "No promises. Just try not to give Jude a reason to reach for his go bag."

Inside, I can hear the sounds of dishes clattering and voices chattering, and my anxiety spikes again. I know my brother's mood well enough to know he's already in a foul mood, and it's only a matter of time before he starts grilling us about our relationship.

Ricca's voice calls out, inviting us in. As we step inside, Jude greets us curtly, his eyes fixed on Lucas. "Well, well, well," he says, his voice dripping with sarcasm. "Look who decided to grace us with his presence. About fucking time."

I roll my eyes at his comment, but Lucas returns the glare with a steely stare. Lucas pulls me into a tight embrace, his warm breath tickling the nape of my neck. Great. Territorial male posturing. If they keep this up, we're going to go nowhere fast.

"Ignore him." Ricca smiles as she passes with a plate of steaming food in her hands. "Table's set and the food is ready. Let's dig in before someone we know starts his third degree before we eat."

We head for the small dinner table in their kitchen, and I notice there's an open space.

"Where's Asher?" I whisper to Ricca.

"Abigail took him to see a movie with Beth and Carter. I thought it would be best if he weren't here to see this."

"He's that mad?"

"Honey, you have no idea. Hope Slider is ready for this."

As we sit at the dinner table, the tension between

Jude and Lucas simmering just below the surface is easily felt. My brother leans back in his chair, his eyes fixed on Lucas. "So," he begins, his tone rough. "When did this shit with my little sister start?"

"Jesus, Jude. I haven't even taken a bite of dinner yet," I jump in before Lucas can even open his mouth. "It's delicious, by the way, Ricca."

My sister-in-law nods her head in silent thanks.

"How long?" he demands again.

"I told you…" I start before my brother glares in my direction.

"Let. Him. Answer." He enunciates each word.

Lucas straightens in his chair next to me. "We were casually seeing each other before I went to prison."

While we may not have solidified our relationship or come to any kind of understanding before everything went to hell, the feelings were very much there.

Jude's eyes narrow. "And I'm just hearing about this now?"

"I told you from the beginning," I snap back, frustration finally getting the best of me. "You obviously weren't listening."

Lucas' hand brushes against mine under the table, a silent gesture of support. I take a deep breath, knowing this will be a long night.

"Do you always let my sister talk for you?" Jude's accusatory tone stings us both.

Lucas' jaw clenches, but he takes a deep breath before responding, "No, I don't. I'm quite capable of speaking for myself, but I respect your sister, and I don't want to say anything that might upset her. I also don't see the need to argue and fight about this when she and I are already together." His words come out measured, but I can hear the underlying frustration in his voice. The anger bubbling just beneath the surface is palpable, and his grip on it is slipping slowly.

Jude doesn't seem to be satisfied with the answer, however. "That's very considerate of you," he drawls. "But I don't think you need to worry about upsetting her. My sister can handle herself just fine."

"I know she can," Lucas says calmly.

"You should have asked me for permission before you started pursuing my sister."

"What is this, the 1950s?" I interject, clearly fed up with Jude's attitude. "I'm not some piece of property that needs your permission. For fuck's sake, Jude, I'm not a teenager. I don't need permission to fuck someone."

My brother's mouth twists into a sneer. "Watch your language, little sister."

"I'm not your little sister," I snap back. "And I'll talk however the fuck I want."

Jude stands up from the table, his eyes blazing with anger. He storms out of the room, and I push away from the table. "Excuse me," I mutter to Ricca and Lucas as I stalk away, hot on my brother's heels.

If he wants to be an asshole, fine, but I will not put up with him disrespecting my relationship or my choices. This fight he's picking isn't about my relationship or gaining his permission. There's something else going on.

"Well, that was certainly welcoming for our first family dinner," I chastise Jude when I find him outside, pacing in the backyard.

He stops pacing, turning to face me with a hard expression. "What do you want me to do? Accept this with open arms?" he says, his voice low and menacing.

"Yes," I admit.

"I won't."

"What's really going on here, Jude? Why are you so against our relationship." I step toward him. "I thought you, of all people, would be happy I found someone you know you can trust. Someone who will keep me close to home."

Jude's jaw clenches as he takes a deep breath, the muscles in his neck bulging with the effort to keep his emotions in check. "It's not about trust, Ginny," he says, his voice dripping with frustration. "It's about the kind of world he comes from. The world I come from. It's not safe for you to be associated with the kind of life we lead."

"It's safe for Ricca and Asher. But not me?" I fire back. My simmering frustration with my brother taking over. "Why them and not me?"

"Because of what you've been through already," he roars. "It's safer for you to lead a normal life. Not tying yourself to one of our members."

"Why don't you let me be the judge of that?" I step closer to my brother. "You've been protecting me my entire life, Jude. It's time you let me go. If I'm going to make my own mistakes, you have to let me." I step closer, allowing him to see the determination in my eyes. "I want to see where this goes with him. Jude, I love him."

My brother stills in front of me, his face unreadable. "It's not the life I want for you."

"But that's just it. It's *my* life. Let *me* live it."

"You're asking me to let you go when I just got you back," Jude admits. "I've always protected you, Ginny. It's my job."

"It's *his* job now," I remind him. "Lucas is a good man. Knowing he was waiting for me is what got me through the last four years, Jude. We got each other through it. Maybe I should have spelled it out more clearly when I came back at Christmas, but I want this life with him and the club. They're my family. Our family now."

Jude's eyes soften as he takes in my words. "I just don't want to see you hurt," he says, his voice low and pained. "You're my baby sister."

"I know," I reply, stepping closer and wrapping my arms around his waist. "But I'm not a baby anymore."

He hesitates for a moment before he wraps his arms around me in return. "You will always be my baby sister, Ginny." My brother shakes his head. "You're wrong about something, though. It will *always* be my job to look out for you. I'm just letting him try it out on a trial run."

"So does that mean you'll let him live?"

"We'll see."

I pull away from Jude, rolling my eyes at his dramatics. "He's not going to hurt me, Jude. I promise."

He nods, seeming to accept my words. "All right, Ginny. If you're sure about this, then I'll back off." He pauses for a moment, looking me over with a scrutinizing gaze. "But you'd better be damn sure about this because if anything happens to you, it'll be on my head."

"I understand," I say, reaching for his hand and giving it a reassuring squeeze. "I'm sure, Jude. I really am."

He nods again, letting out a sigh. "All right then. I'll think about it." Jude releases me, a hint of a smile on his lips as he steps back. "Don't thank me yet. You still have a lot to prove."

I nod, determination settling in my gut. I will prove to him that I can handle this life—being with Lucas, part of the club, and a valuable member in my own right.

As we make our way back into the house, Lucas' eyes meet mine, and I can see the relief in his expression. I reach for his hand, lacing our fingers together. It's not going to be easy, but I know we can make it work. We have to.

"This was supposed to be a nice family dinner," Ricca mutters under her breath as we take our seats at the table once again.

"It's all right," I say, squeezing Lucas' hand.

Lucas meets my gaze, and the love and understanding emanating in his eyes almost overwhelms me. We'll get through this together.

As we continue our dinner, the tension in the air slowly dissipates. We talk about unimportant things, trying to keep the mood light. But I sense this won't be the last time we have a conversation like this with my brother.

I'm ready for it, though.

I'm ready to fight for what I want and believe in.

And I know Lucas will always be by my side, ready to fight with me.

We're in this together.

Chapter 13

SLIDER

"WHERE ARE YOU GOING?" Ginny's sleepy voice cuts through the early morning fog as I tug on my jeans at the end of the bed.

I turn around and face her, taking a moment to admire her natural beauty—how her freckles perfectly align across her nose and cheeks and her lips purse slightly as she waits for my response. Her dark, messy bun atop her head sticks up in every direction. "Come back to bed." She pats her hand on my side of the bed.

"I have a meeting, Gin," I say with a smile, walking over to her. Ginny's hands reach out of the covers, gliding up my thighs before her fingers slip into my waistband, tugging me onto the bed on top of her.

"You could miss it, right?"

I lean in, pressing my lips gently onto her freckled nose, then down her lips, savoring the taste of her sweet breath. "I can't miss this one, baby," I murmur against her lips. Truthfully, I want to miss it, but I have a limited window to try to satisfy Smith.

Ginny's tongue ventures out to meet mine as we engage in a slow, languid kiss that sends waves of pleasure coursing through my veins.

Ginny's hands wander down my back, pulling me closer to her as she deepens the kiss. We break apart for a moment, catching our breaths as Ginny's hands slowly trail down to my hips. She looks up at me, her eyes heavy with desire, and my dick's hard at the thought of what we could do right now.

"I'd rather spend my morning with you," I confess, my voice rough with emotion.

Ginny's hands are still on my hips while she looks up at me with a mischievous grin. "Then don't go," she murmurs, reaching down to stroke my length through my jeans.

I gasp, my eyes rolling back in pleasure as I feel her warm hand on me. "Ginny," I moan, leaning my forehead against hers.

"Let me make it worth your while," she whispers, pulling me down and then rolling on top of me. Her hips straddling my waist.

She giggles and squirms under my touch, causing

my desire to grow. I hold her tighter, feeling her body press against mine. This might put me behind schedule, but I can't help but take a moment to savor her.

Smith and his damn deadline can wait another hour.

Ginny's lips meet mine, melting away any remaining resistance as I surrender to the moment. There is nowhere I'd rather be right now than here in her arms.

"I like this," I admit. My hands moving to her waist above me.

"This?" she teases, grinding her bare pussy against my jeans.

"Fuck, Gin." I hiss. My hands cup her ass, bringing her pussy to my face. She squeals until my tongue licks a line up her pussy, relaxing her hips around my head as I devour her. Ginny gasps, her muscles clenching around my tongue as I drink her in, her sweet nectar dripping down my chin.

I lay a light bite on her clit. She squirms, trying to shift, but my hands drag her more tightly against me. The headboard shifts behind my head as she grasps it for leverage.

Ginny's orgasm builds quickly, her hips thrusting against my mouth. I feel her pleasure coursing through her veins, begging for her release. With one final lick, she comes undone around me, her hips clenching around my head.

Ginny swings her hips over my head, collapsing next to me, her chest heaving from her release. She reaches out, sliding her hands under my waistband, cupping my aching cock.

"The things that you do to me, Gin."

"There are a few more things I'd like to do this morning," she admits with a coy smile.

I curl my arm around her, pulling Ginny close into my chest. She giggles, stretching her body out with a satisfied sigh. I brush the hair away from her face as we lay tangled together.

I glance down at the clock, regretting that I need to leave but knowing I must. V had mentioned Presley having an appointment for the baby this morning, bitching about how early it was so Presley didn't have to change her schedule at her practice. I'd already planned to poke around his office, and this provided me with the perfect opportunity—V is gone, and everyone else is still asleep.

"I could stay here forever," I murmur in Ginny's ear, my eyes closed.

She smiles and kisses my cheek. "Me too," she says, trailing her fingers lightly over my chest.

I turn to face her, propping myself up on my elbow. "Unfortunately, I have to go." I groan, pressing my forehead against hers. I want to stay, but I know I have to leave—fulfilling my obligations not just to Smith but also to myself is imperative.

She leans in to kiss me softly, and I know she's trying to persuade me to stay. It almost works, but I eventually pull away, regretfully. "I really do have to go," I say, standing up from the bed and grabbing my T-shirt. My throbbing cock is protesting the decision the second my feet hit the floor.

Ginny watches as I get dressed, her eyes following my every movement.

"I won't be long. We can pick up where we left off when I get back."

Ginny gives me a small smile. "Okay, I'll be waiting," she says, laying her head on the pillow.

I pause for a moment, admiring how beautiful she looks, before I lean in and kiss her one final time. "I love you," I whisper, pulling away.

Ginny's face breaks out in a big grin. "I love you too," she says softly as I walk away, her words echoing in my ears as I close the door behind me.

The clubhouse is quiet, as I thought it would be. Early mornings are the least populated time as most of the guys live off-site with their families. I'd only really seen Thor and two new prospects I haven't met yet around after most people left for the day. A drastic change since I'd gone to prison.

Quietly walking down the hallway, I purposely

keep my footsteps light as I walk toward the offices on the other side of the common room—no need to draw unnecessary attention to myself. I pretend to stretch, stopping by the bar to grab a water from the mini refrigerator. V has cameras everywhere in the main spaces. So I need to be aware to not gain his attention if he reviews the footage later. For all he knows, I'm up early, and not trying to steal the club's secrets to keep Smith's target off Ginny's back.

I casually drink the bottle of water before discarding it and walking out of the room toward the hallway of offices. I pass V's first, the door slightly open, and peek inside. On the far wall, his computer setups hum on the long desk. A series of monitors hang on the wall above them. I peer over my shoulder, listening for any moment before I slip into the office.

Making sure to keep the door in its original position, I take my time crossing over to the computers and gaze at the monitors. Dozens of camera feeds reveal the main room, the outside of the building, and the outbuildings. Nothing's stirring.

Heading to the desk, I turn my attention to the computer. I move the mouse, and the screen clicks on with a password prompt.

Shit. I attempt a few guesses, but nothing works. I knew his computer was a long shot anyway. He always kept it locked up tighter than Fort Knox, but I had to try. There are a few papers on his desk—invoices for new equipment and some unreadable scribbles—but nothing of use for me here.

Fuck. Running my hands through my hair, I sigh. Smith's deadline is today. If I don't come up with something, he could move on Ginny. I scan the room, hoping and praying there is something I am not seeing. Something hiding in plain sight, but there's nothing.

As I am about to stand up from the chair, I hear the front door open. Everyone's still asleep, and I thought I was alone. It could be a prospect coming to clean or a delivery, but I need to be careful. With my heart pounding in my chest, I wait to see who it is on the security screens above me.

The door opens, and Hero walks into the common room. My stomach drops. This could be bad. I take a few deep breaths, trying to control my inner panic. I have to get out of here without him noticing.

Hero starts to move around the room, humming a tune as he goes. I try to replace the paperwork I'd touched on V's desk neatly and correctly. My hands stack the papers before something shifts below them as I peer down.

A flash drive.

Fuck. Anything could be on it. It could be a porn

stash for all I know, but I have to bring something to Smith—anything that will keep Ginny safe. My heart hammers in my chest, and I quickly pocket the drive.

I watch as Hero starts toward this hallway. My eyes widen, and I know now I am stuck. I'm out of time and options. I look around. There's no way out. I'm about to be busted.

The heavy thuds of Hero's riding boots echo down the hallway as he walks toward the offices. His office is right next to V's. Shit. Shit. *Shit.* He stops outside V's office, but thankfully, he doesn't open the door. I hear him pause, his boots shifting on the hard-wood floors, but he continues. Then I hear the door unlatch next door, and his footsteps head inside the room.

I release the breath I had been holding. A rush of relief passes over me, and I take my chance. Creeping out of the office, I tiptoe back down the hallway with the drive in my pocket, confident I have something to help Smith. The guilt of what I'm doing is eating me alive, and the betrayal of my club is becoming more real with the flash drive burning a hole in my pocket.

Doing this will keep Ginny safe.

I have to focus on that and not the guilt.

I make it down the hallway when Hero's voice calls out to me.

"Thought I heard someone out here," he says from his office doorway.

I turn around, trying to put on an innocent face, prepared to lie my ass off to protect the club and Ginny.

"Oh hey, there," I say, forcing a smile.

He looks me up and down, one eyebrow slightly raised. "You're up early," he states.

I shrug. "Yeah, couldn't sleep." I smile, hoping my cover story is believable. "Thought I'd grab breakfast for Ginny."

"Hmm," he hums, still suspicious. "Heard you had dinner with Ratchet last night. Glad to see you're still alive." Hero smiles finally.

"It wasn't exactly a walk in the park," I admit. "It got pretty dicey there for a while."

"He'll come around," Hero reassures me. "If V is still living after shacking up with Raze's sister, I'm sure Ratch will too."

"Fuck, I hope so."

"Trust me, Slider. It'll work itself out. Always does."

I wish I could trust what he was saying, but if he knew the contents of my pocket at this moment, he would be the first one to take my life.

"I'm gonna head out," I declare.

Hero steps aside, giving me a nod, and I quickly

slip past him out the door. I don't dare look back, holding my breath until I'm out of sight. I head outside toward my bike. I'd told Hero about getting breakfast for Ginny, and I know I have to keep up the ruse not to draw his suspicion. Mounting my bike, I pull out my Smith-provided cell phone and fire off a text.

> Found a flash drive.

He responds immediately.

> What's on it?

> Don't know.

> Find out.

I sigh heavily.

I don't know what I'll find on the drive, but one thing I do know—it will change everything.

Chapter 14

GINNY

"COME ON, ASHER!" Ricca screams from beside me in the bleachers as Beth passes the ball to him, maneuvering it between his feet. The other team's enforcer is hot on his tail. He shifts his body toward the left before abruptly cutting right. The enforcer is caught off guard, and Asher bolts toward the goal and kicks.

The ball soars through the air, narrowly going through the goalie's fanned hands before hitting the net.

"Goal!" the announcer yells over the loud, cheering crowd. The ear-ringing cheers and catcalls from the surrounding audience dissipate into white noise as I focus my attention on Asher and his wide smile as he waves to Ricca and me from the pitch. They start back down toward the other end when the

referee blows his whistle once time runs out with Asher's team ahead by two goals.

His team runs toward the center of the field, circling him. The team celebrates their win before shaking hands with their opponents.

Ricca shifts next to me, gathering her belongings.

Asher bounds up, his smile a mile wide.

"Did you see my goal?" he asks his sister. "Awesome, right?"

Ricca rolls her eyes before pushing past him. "Yeah, yeah. It was okay," she says, feigning disinterest. But I can see the sparkle in her eyes, the same one mirrored in Asher's.

"Don't listen to her," I mutter. "You did great."

A few of his teammates call out for him, and he pivots to join them on the sidelines.

"Any big plans after the game today?" I ask her. Due to helping with the security firm, she's barely made it to Asher's last few games.

"I'm sure he'll try to convince me to get ice cream since you always take him after games."

"Whoops?" I smile. "What's wrong with a victory treat?"

Ricca shakes her head, her smile widening. "Nothing, you spoil him too much."

I chuckle before standing up from the bleachers.

"Well, I have to spoil him a little. After all, he's my favorite guy."

Ricca nods before turning to look at her brother. "Come on, Asher! We're going to get ice cream."

Asher runs over, his eyes wide with excitement. "Yes! Can we go to that new place that has the giant sundaes?"

Ricca side-eyes me. "I may have promised him we'd go after this game."

"Fine." She scoffs. "Is Beth coming too?"

Asher turns around, flashing a thumbs up to Beth and her sister, Abigail, who are not far behind him. We start toward the parking lot.

"Are you joining us?" Ricca asks.

"Sure. I'll text Slider to see if he wants to meet us there."

We say our goodbyes. Ricca heads off toward the other side of the parking lot where she'd parked her SUV with Beth and Abigail in tow. With so many games going on in the park today, I ended up parking in the outer lot away from everyone else, thanks to Lucas making me late.

I make my way to my car, digging my keys out of my pocket. Ricca and Abigail honk as they pass me, and I wave at them. I'm only a few feet away from my car when I notice that my front end seems to be lower to the ground. I approach closer to find that the passenger side tire is flat as two-day-old road kill.

"Shit," I curse. "How in the hell did that happen?" I crouch down, inspecting it. A large gash on the sidewall hisses with escaping air. My fingers trace it, the cut a few inches wide.

I let out a sigh and stand, leaning against my car. I'm not exactly sure how to change a tire, but I know I will have to figure it out. I peer over, noticing that the back tire is also hissing.

I walk around to the driver's side and find both of those tires are also flat. What the hell did I hit? One flat tire, I could deal with the spare in the trunk, but four? Shit. One spare isn't going to fix this, and magically having a set of four spares in the trunk is not going to happen. I pull out my cell from my pocket, clicking Lucas' name to call him. It rings, and as I stare at the tire, contemplating how we're going to manage this, I hear footsteps approaching me from behind.

"Need some help?" a deep, commanding voice says. I turn, my phone drawn against my ear, to find Roman standing there. My phone drops from my ear, hitting the ground with a thud.

My heart races, and my breathing quickens as Roman steps closer. He towers over me, his muscular frame and chiseled features almost too much to take in. He reaches out and picks up my phone, handing it to me with a smile. "Are you okay?" he asks, his voice sending shivers down my spine.

"I, uh, yeah. I just have a flat tire. Four, actually," I reply, gesturing toward my car.

Roman takes a closer look at the tires before nodding. "Looks like it. You got a spare?"

"Just one."

Roman follows my gaze, his brow furrowing. "That's not good."

"Tell me about it," I joke, trying not to draw attention to my unease at his reappearance. "Just my luck, huh?"

"Did you hit something on your way here?"

"I don't think so." My car is newer, a gift from my brother when I came back. If I'd hit something, the low-pressure sensors would have alerted me, or so I thought they would. His predatory gaze unsettles me. Lucas' words echo in my head, *If Roman ever approached me again. Call him immediately.*

Roman's lips twist into a smirk. "Well, let's take a closer look and see what we're working with." He kneels beside me, inspecting the punctured tires. As he runs his hand over the gash, I can feel the warmth of his body radiating toward me, an unsettling feeling that he's so close to me.

"Do you know how to change a tire?" I ask, trying to break the near-silent tension between us.

He chuckles. "Yeah, I know how to change a tire. But with four flats, it's not going to be much help. We'll have to call for a tow truck."

"I can do that." Drawing up my phone, I pretend to search for local tow companies but instead use the opportunity to text Lucas.

> At the soccer field. Roman's here.
> Tires slashed. I'm alone.

He calls me immediately.

Thankfully, my phone is silent without the vibration option on. I draw up my phone to my ear.

"Yeah, hi. I have four flat tires at Rancho Park, and I need a tow."

"Is he still there?" Lucas growls into the receiver, immediately catching on to what I'm doing.

"Yes, that's right. Four flats."

"Can you get away from him?"

"No, I'm in the gravel lot by the soccer fields," I answer. My heart pounds in my chest, and I pray he doesn't realize what I'm doing.

"I'm coming, baby," he assures me. "Keep the line open and on you if he tries to take you. V can track it."

"Yeah, that's fine. My insurance should cover the

cost." I step away from Roman, trying to put more distance between us while desperately trying to keep up my ruse.

"If you can keep him there, I'll take care of it, but if he tries to do anything, run, Ginny. Run and don't look back."

"Please hurry. I'm supposed to be meeting my family for ice cream, and I don't want to miss it."

"Hang tight, baby. I'm on my way." The roar of his bike's engine muffles his voice.

Roman pushes up from the ground. His body is way too close to mine. I take a step back, trying to put some distance between us.

"Any luck?" he asks.

"Yeah, they said they could have someone out here soon." I mute the line before sliding my phone with the call to Lucas still connected into my back pocket, away from his prying eyes.

"You know, we could wait for the tow truck together," he suggests, a smirk playing on his lips.

I swallow hard, trying to ignore the uneasy feeling in my gut. "I don't think that's necessary. I can wait alone."

"Oh, come on. It's not safe for a pretty lady like you to be out here all alone," he says, taking a step closer to me.

"I'm fine," I reply, taking a step back. "I'll just wait in my car."

Roman takes another step toward me, his eyes flickering with something I can't quite place. "I'll wait with you. Wouldn't want anyone to try and take advantage of you while you're stranded out here."

"I appreciate the offer, really…" I say, trying to keep my voice steady, "… but I can take care of myself. And besides, you have places to be, right? I'm sure you'd rather watch your daughter's game than stand out here in the hot sun with me."

His brow arches at the mention of his daughter before he chuckles. "I can spare a little time for a damsel in distress."

"Who did they play today?"

"Whose team?" he fires back.

"Your daughter's."

"Oh right. She didn't have a game today. She's with her mother this week." The blatant lie rolls easily from his lips. *Is the girl even his daughter?* The convenience of our chance meeting is beginning to appear more planned than by chance.

"Then why are you here?" I ask, trying to ease the tension between us.

"I was hoping to run into you again."

My stomach drops. "You wanted to run into me? Why?" I coyly answer.

"After the last game, I was kicking myself for not asking for your number and asking you out. Figured you'd be back to watch another game, so I checked the schedule to see when your nephew, was it, played again."

"Oh, I'm flattered that you came all this way to see me, but I'm seeing someone."

"Ah, I see," he says, his eyes gleaming with something that makes me even more uneasy. "Well, he's a lucky guy."

I nod, not sure what else to say. The air between us thickens with an almost palpable tension, and I feel my heart racing.

"He in your brother's club?" he asks.

"Yeah," I nod. "Just patched in, actually."

"Interesting guys, the Heaven's Rejects. I'm surprised someone like you would associate with them."

"Like me?" I gulp again, my eyes scanning for an escape route or another person walking near us. Lucas has to be close by now.

"Yeah, you seem like a sweet girl. Not the type to run with a motorcycle club."

I force a smile. "Looks can be deceiving, I guess."

Roman takes another step closer, his breath hot on my neck. "I like deceiving looks," he murmurs, reaching out to touch my hair.

I flinch away from his touch. "Please don't touch me."

"Relax, I'm not going to hurt you," he says, but there's an edge to his voice that makes me doubt his words.

My heart pounds in my chest as I consider my options. I could try to make a break for it, but Roman is bigger and stronger than me. Or I could wait for Lucas to arrive, but I don't know how long that will take.

"Come on," Roman says, his hand on my arm now. "Let's go back to my car. I have some drinks in the cooler. We can wait for the tow truck there."

The fear in my stomach turns to ice. I pull away from him, shaking my head. "I'm fine here. The tow truck will arrive soon."

Roman's smile fades, replaced by a scowl. "You don't have a choice, sweetheart. I have orders to bring you with me."

Orders? Why would anyone want me?

I freeze, the color draining from my face. How did he know about that? I had made sure to cover my tracks.

"I don't know w-what you're t-talking about," I stammer, trying to pull away from him again.

"Oh, I think you do," he growls, his grip tightening on my waist. "But lucky for you, my boss wants you alive."

"Let me go!" I scream, hoping someone will hear me.

But this side of the park is empty as I shove at his hands.

"No, can do, sweetheart. I'm going to make a pretty penny when I deliver you to my boss. You cost him millions with your little fucking stunt with the Zezza family."

I freeze, my mind racing as I try to process his words. Zezza family? What the hell did he mean? I try to pull away from him, but he's too strong. My heart races as he starts dragging me toward his car.

But then, I hear the roar of a motorcycle in the distance. Hope surges through my veins as I realize that Lucas has finally arrived. I struggle harder to break free from Roman's grip, but he's so strong.

I'm about to give up when Lucas' bike roars into view. He pulls up alongside us and revs his engine, eyeing Roman warily.

Roman sneers at him.

Lucas doesn't answer. Instead, he dismounts his bike and walks over to me, his eyes flickering with concern. "You put those marks on her?" Lucas growls, eyeing the marks left on my arms from his grasp.

Lucas steps in front of us, blocking him from the car behind him, his eyes locked on Roman's.

"You shouldn't have touched what's mine."

Roman snorts. "And who says she's yours?"

Lucas' eyes flash dangerously. "I do."

Before he can say anything, Lucas charges for me. His hands grasp mine as he shoves me out of Roman's hold and toward the ground, the gravel biting as it jabs into my exposed arms.

Lucas punches him in the face. Roman stumbles back, clutching his nose as blood oozes down around his mouth. He tries to retaliate, but Lucas is far too quick for him. He punches him again, and this time, Roman falls to the ground.

I watch in horror as the fight unfolds before me, unsure of what to do. Part of me wants to run away, but I know I can't leave Lucas to fight this guy alone. So I stay put and watch as Slider delivers blow after blow to Roman.

Finally, he lands a final punch on Roman's chin, and he crumples to the ground, unconscious.

Lucas approaches me, his eyes softening as they meet mine.

"Are you okay?" he asks, his voice gentle.

I nod, my heart racing in my chest. "I think so."

"Fuck, Gin. I thought I'd lost you. If I had been a minute later, you'd be gone."

"But you weren't. I'm here safe with you." All I see is him standing in front of me, strong and protective. "You came for me."

"I will *always* come for you, Gin."

The roar of two more motorcycles speeding into the parking lot draws my attention. My brother and Thor skid to a stop next to us.

Jude rushes to me, checking me all over.

"I'm fine," I reassure him.

"I'll fucking kill him," he snarls, looking over to where Roman is still unconscious by my car with Thor standing over him.

"Get in fucking line," Lucas interjects.

"Take her home," my brother orders. "I'll take care of this. Get Doc to check her out."

With a final glance at my brother and Thor, Lucas starts his bike and drives away from the scene. I hold onto him tightly, feeling a mix of relief and fear. I have never been in a situation like this before.

As we ride away, Lucas keeps a steady pace, but I feel the tension in his body. I know he's trying to keep his cool for my sake. His grip on the handlebars tightens, and the muscles in his back tense.

I lean in closer, resting my head against his back. "Thank you," I whisper.

Lucas nods, but he doesn't say anything.

Chapter 15

SLIDER

"HOW IS SHE?" Raze asks when I join the club in one of our outbuildings.

"Shaken up, but fine. Doc's with her now."

As much as I want to be with her, my place is here.

"Where the fuck were you?" Ratchet hisses when he notices me. "You were supposed to be with her."

"I was caught up at the clubhouse," I lie. "I was going to meet her there after the game. It was broad daylight. She should have been fine."

"She fucking wasn't," he snarls.

"Don't you think I know that?" Seeing her so vulnerable, his hands all over her, dragging her to his car, replays repeatedly in my mind. I try to push the image away, but it haunts me like a ghost. The anger inside me boiling like a volcano about to erupt. "I made a mistake."

I was supposed to be with her at the game. I was supposed to be her guardian, and I fucking failed her. All because I needed her out of our room to try to access that fucking flash drive, a feat that was a failure.

"That mistake could have cost her life. Remember that the next time you think whatever it is you are doing is more important than Ginny."

He's right. This is my fault. The blame for everything now and coming our way is squarely on me.

Ratchet storms away from me while all the eyes of the club are on me after the loud exchange.

"Is he awake?" Raze asks as Thor dumps Roman into the steel chair in Ratchet's workshop. He groans, but his eyes remain closed.

"Not yet," he answers.

Thor strips him of his cut, tossing it to Raze, who catches it with one hand. He flips it to the back. The Twisted Tribe rocker and colors are on full display in front of us, confirmation of what Ginny had told Ratchet about her first encounter with him.

Our long-dead rivals are back in the land of the living.

Raze shows the rest of the guys the cut before tossing it on the floor.

"Not fucking possible," Hero snarls. "No one left that safe house."

"That cut says otherwise," Raze declares. "Do it," he orders Ratchet.

"Secure him," Ratchet demands. Thor retrieves a heavy chain from the far wall of the building, the metal clanging with each step like a death rattle. As Thor wraps a long chain around Roman's chest and legs, Ratchet walks over to his workbench and picks up a pair of pliers. He tests the sharp edges with his finger, maliciously grinning as he strides back to Roman's restrained form.

"Time to wake up, asshole," Ratchet says, gripping Roman's hand with the pliers. Roman's eyes flutter open, and he groans in pain.

"What the hell is going on?" he slurs, his eyes struggling to focus on Ratchet's face.

"I'm gonna ask the questions," Ratchet says, squeezing the pliers.

Roman's eyes widen with fear as he realizes his precarious position.

Ratchet releases his grip and leans in closer. "Why did you try to take the girl?"

Roman squirms in his chair, trying to find an escape. "I don't know what you're talking about," he says unconvincingly.

Ratchet's nostrils flare with rage, and he slams the

pliers onto the table. "Don't fuck with me," he growls. "It won't save you."

Roman swallows hard, his face twisted in fear. "I was assigned to watch her," he stammers.

"Assigned?"

This couldn't be Smith, could it? Why would he hire another MC to watch her? He has everything at his disposal. This doesn't make fucking sense at all.

Roman shifts, wincing at the pain in his mangled finger. "Yes," he stutters. "Someone wanted to know where she is at all times."

I rake my hand over my face, trying to conceal the look I know I am wearing. *Goddammit! This has Smith written all over it.*

"And why do they want her?" Ratchet prompts, his voice dangerously low.

Roman blinks rapidly. It's clear he's trying to figure out what to say. He takes a deep breath. "I don't know," he insists. "The payment was good, and I wanted the money. I didn't ask questions."

Ratchet stares at him for a long moment, then turns to the rest of us. "We need to figure out who hired this asshole," he says. He turns back to Roman. "You're gonna help us," he orders.

Roman's face pales, and he shakes his head fervently. "I can't," he replies.

"Can't?" Ratchet laughs. "Can't isn't going to

keep you alive. You'll answer my questions. For each one you refuse, you lose something. In fact, I think you need to understand how serious I am." Ratchet steps away, replacing the pliers on the workbench and grabbing a pair of steel cutters. He places the sharp blades around the knuckle of Roman's left pointer finger and squeezes. He screams as his finger severs, falling to the floor with blood pouring from the wound. The smell of oil, steel, and broken bones mingle with fear and desperation as piss streaks down the legs of his jeans.

Roman looks at Ratchet fearfully, his body trembling. "Next, I take something a little more important." Ratchet's eyes fall to Roman's groin. "Do you understand?" Ratchet asks, his voice terse.

Roman nods his head slowly. "Yes," he whispers.

Ratchet stands and begins to walk away. "Good," he says over his shoulder. "Now tell us what you know. Tell us who hired you. Where are the rest of your Twisted Tribe buddies?"

Roman shakes his head, tears dripping down his face. "My club?" he mutters. "I'm not in a club."

Raze grabs the cut from the floor, shoving it in his face. "Then why the fuck are you wearing Twisted Tribes' colors?"

"Part of the job."

We all look to Raze. "Explain," he orders. The cut still tightly gripped in his hand.

"I don't know, motherfucker," he spits out, pain still lacing his words.

Ratchet picks up a wrench from the bench and hefts it in his hand. Roman's eyes widen, and he starts to shake his head, but Ratchet clamps a hand around his throat and slams the wrench into his chest. Roman cries out in pain, but Ratchet doesn't let go.

"Answer the question," he says coldly. "Now."

Roman lets out a shuddering breath, his lips trembling as he speaks. "It came with the money and an order to wear it. "They said they wanted someone who could blend in. Someone who could move about without raising any suspicion."

"Say I believe you," Ratchet offers, circling him. "What did they want you to do with the girl?"

"Keep her until they called."

Ratchet looks to the rest of us. I can see the anger swelling in his eyes. "For what?"

"The mole," Roman murmurs. "They needed an insurance policy."

I still. My stomach churns with fear and anger. The rest of the club exchanges glances. A few eyes fall to me for my reaction.

"Do you know who the mole is?" Ratchet asks.

Fuck! My heart pounds in my chest. This could be it—the end of the line. If Smith has told him my name, I'm dead. Dead before I can fucking fix this and protect Ginny.

Roman shakes his head. "No," he replies. "Just that they'd contact me with what to do with the girl if the mole didn't report back. Rough her up, but keep her alive until they called."

Ratchet stills. His hand clenching the cutters in his hand. He swings hard, his fist and the cutters connecting with the bastard's jaw. Blood spews as Roman's head turns with the force of the blow. Teeth clattering onto the floor next to him.

"Tell. Me. The. Truth." His words land with a corresponding blow.

Roman's head rolls to the side, moans escape his bloodied mouth, and his head limp on his neck. "That's all I know," he forces out, his words muffled with gurgles of blood.

"Then there's no reason I should keep you alive," Ratchet says coldly.

Roman's eyes widen before Ratchet grabs a gun off the workbench and points it at his head. He peers over to Raze, who nods.

"Any last words?"

Roman shakes his head, realizing his fate too late. Ratchet pulls the trigger, the sound of the shot echoing through the warehouse and the smell of blood saturating our noses. His head is tipped back with his brains splattered against the stainless steel wall behind him.

Ratchet stares at Roman's lifeless body before sighing and holstering the gun.

I let out a breath I hadn't realized I was holding, but it doesn't feel like any sort of relief. I can't shake the feeling of guilt, knowing it's my fault this man died.

"Get rid of him and clean up the mess," Raze orders, looking at Ratchet and me. "Make him fucking disappear."

We don't pause or hesitate.

We get to work.

Chapter 16

GINNY

A NIGHTMARE DRAWS me from my sleep. It's the same one I've been having since my attempted abduction and one that hasn't resurfaced since Rigo was sent to prison. My arms flail as I wake, my healing forearm smacking against the bedside table, causing me to hiss in pain. I cradle it against me when Lucas comes running from the bathroom, where I hear the shower running. Water drips from his hair down onto his naked torso and the basketball shorts he has on.

"Are you okay?"

"I'm fine."

I brush off his concern, allowing my fear to mask my embarrassment at being caught off guard by the nightmare. I sit up and swing my legs over the side of the bed, running a hand through my hair. My eyes meet Lucas' in the dim light of the room, and I see the worry etched into his features.

His sculpted muscles tense as he watches me closely, his eyes filled with concern. "You sure?" he asks, his voice deep and soothing.

I nod, biting my lip. My heart is racing, and my mind is still foggy from the nightmare. I hate how vulnerable it makes me feel and question everything around me. Lucas senses my turmoil and wraps an arm around my shoulders, pulling me into his embrace.

"It's okay, Gin," he whispers, pressing his lips to my temple. "I'm here. I'll protect you."

I melt into his touch, finding comfort in his arms—something about his presence calms me and makes the world feel a little less scary. And as I breathe in his scent—a combination of soap, shampoo, and his natural musk—I feel a sense of peace.

He pulls back, searching my eyes. "Do you want to talk about it?"

I shake my head. "Not really."

He nods. "Are you sure? V said Presley will swing by and do your session here today."

"I told you, I'm fine," I snap, my voice coming out more forcefully than I had planned. For a week now, he's hovered, never letting me out of his sight. Roman's attack only left me with mild injuries—cuts to my arms from the gravel and bruising. Lucas had been treating me with kid gloves, constantly hovering like a mother hen. He hasn't touched me once, clearly afraid I will break under his grasp. He's even taken up to sleeping in a chair he dragged in from the main room instead of sharing our bed for fear of hurting me.

"There's no need to make Presley change her schedule for me. I can drive to her office. It'll be fine."

"You're not leaving the clubhouse."

"Excuse me?"

Lucas' expression darkens, and his jaw tightens. "You're *not* leaving the clubhouse until we find out who's behind this. You were almost abducted, Gin. We can't take any chances."

I raise an eyebrow, letting his words sink in. Lucas' protectiveness is both comforting and suffocating. I know he means well, but his overbearing nature is starting to grate on my nerves. "So, what... am I a prisoner now?"

"No, of course not. Just until we figure things out."

I sigh, a wave of frustration washing over me. "And how long is that going to be? Days? Weeks? Months? I'm not going to put my life on hold,

Lucas." His real name rolls off my tongue, and he stills. "If I hide, they win."

"And what if something happens to you?" Lucas' voice rises, his eyes flashing with anger. "What if we can't protect you? What if—"

"I can take care of myself. I've been doing it for years."

"That's not\ the point, Gin. You shouldn't have to."

"I know that, but I also know I can't just sit around, waiting for someone to rescue me. I need to live my life. And if that means taking precautions, then so be it, but I won't be a prisoner."

Lucas' gaze softens, his lips quirking into a gentle smile. "I'm not trying to imprison you, Gin. I only want you safe."

"There's a fine line between protecting and imprisoning me. I spent the last four years of my life under lock and key, away from my family and you. I won't let you lock me up and throw away the key because of an almost."

"That almost could have taken you away from me. Had I been any later, you'd have been gone."

I swallow hard and lock my eyes on his—his words piercing me like a bullet.

I know he means well, but I can't help the feeling he's trying to take away my freedom and independence. It's what I've always fought for—a life without a cage, without being told what to do or where to go. That's what brought me here to the clubhouse—the sense of belonging and being part of something bigger than just myself. But now, with Lucas' protectiveness, it's all starting to feel like a trap.

"I know," I say softly, my voice barely above a whisper. "But, you weren't. I'm not going to let fear control my life. That's not living. That's just... existing."

Lucas nods, his hand brushing a stray strand of hair behind my ear. "I get that. I do. But I can't help wanting to keep you safe. You mean everything to me, Gin. I can't lose you."

He sighs, running a hand through his hair. I can tell he's struggling between his need to protect me and his desire to let me live my life.

"You won't," I promise him. "But you know what it feels like to have your freedom stripped away from you too. That helpless feeling as you watch the world go on without you from the window of your cell. Please, Lucas, don't do this to me. Don't lock me away like a priceless possession."

Lucas' eyes soften as he gazes at me, and I can see the love I've come to know so well shining through them. "I'm sorry, Gin," he whispers. "You're right. I just… I can't stand the thought of something happening to you."

"I know," I reply softly, taking his hand in mine. "And I appreciate everything you've done to keep me safe, but I need to be able to make my own decisions and live my life on my terms."

"I understand," Lucas says, his tone gentle. "I'll back off a bit, but promise me you'll be careful. That you won't take any unnecessary risks."

"I promise," I reply, squeezing his hand. "And I'll make you a deal. You let me live my life, and I'll let you protect me… within reason."

"Deal," Lucas agrees, a smile spreading across his face. He leans in and kisses me softly, his lips warm and tender against mine—our first kiss in over a week. I lean into it, trying to take more from him, desperate for the intimacy he's denied me.

"I'll let you go where you need to go, but promise me, you'll take someone with you… me, your brother, one of the guys until this is over, baby. You need protection if you're going to leave."

I nod, knowing his request is fair and reasonable. I don't want to put myself in unnecessary danger, and having someone with me will make me feel safer. "Okay," I agree. "I'll take someone with me wherever I go."

"Good," Lucas says, his smile widening. "And

now that we've got that sorted out, why don't we go back to bed and make up for lost time?"

I can't help but grin at the suggestion, feeling a spark of desire ignite in my chest. It's been too long since we've been intimate, and I'm craving his touch.

"Sounds like a plan," I reply.

Lucas' hands roam over my body, eliciting shivers of pleasure as he kisses my neck and collarbone. I moan softly as he takes one of my nipples into his mouth, his tongue teasing it until it's hard and sensitive.

"God, I've missed you," Lucas murmurs against my skin, his fingers sliding between my thighs. I gasp as he finds my clit, his touch sending shock-waves of pleasure through me.

"Whose fault is that?" I reply, my head spinning with a mix of desire and need. It feels like forever since we've been this close, and I never want it to end. "I've been in this bed for a week while you slept in your chair."

"I was trying to give you space."

"I didn't want space, asshole. I wanted you."

"It's my fault," Lucas admits, his touches becoming increasingly urgent.

"Then make it up to me," I whisper, my hips thrusting against his hand. He chuckles softly, the sound sending shivers down my spine.

"Anything you want, Gin." He purrs, his lips claiming mine in a passionate kiss. "Just say the word."

"Word."

Lucas grins, his eyes blazing with desire. "Then I guess I better make you scream my name."

Chapter 17

SLIDER

SMITH'S PHONE begins to ring inside the drawer of my bedside table just before dawn. I swear under my breath. This is the last thing I need this early in the morning. The sun is barely peeking through the window above us. How goddamn early is it? The clock on my table reads five.

Motherfucker.

I peer over to Ginny's sleeping form. Her dark hair is sticking out from under the covers. As it continues to vibrate, she doesn't move, still fast asleep.

Slipping from bed and grabbing the phone from its spot, I head for the bathroom. I turn on the shower to help muffle the conversation.

"What?" My voice is low but firm.

"Good morning to you too, Mr. Sterling."

I lean against the bathroom counter, rubbing my eyes with one hand and holding the phone with the other. "What the fuck do you want?"

"Progress, Mr. Sterling. That's what I want."

"I'm doing the best I can," I admit. The flash drive had proven to be a problem, not surprising considering how good of a hacker V is. If it had been easy, I would have been suspicious. With the situation with Roman, it's a miracle V hadn't noticed it's missing. Touch one of his action figures, only moving it a centimeter and the asshole notices. "It's not that simple."

"That's not good enough. I want my information. *Now*. I've given you enough time to crack that flash drive. Maybe it's time you send it to me."

Sending him the flash drive is the last thing I want to do. Without knowing what exactly is on it, I could inherently give him information to damn us all. I don't want to funnel him information as it is, but if I can control what he gets, it buys me time to figure out how to maneuver out of this mess and keep the club and Ginny safe.

"No."

"What the hell do you mean, *no*? I'm not sure you understand the terms of our deal, Mr. Sterling."

I run a hand through my hair, the water from the shower beginning to steam up the small bathroom.

"I'm still working on it. It may be nothing. Why would I waste your time with that?"

"You're already wasting my time. You've been there for two weeks, and what do I have to show for it? Nothing." He sighs heavily into the phone, and is not wrong to be frustrated. "I don't tolerate incompetence."

"And I don't tolerate attempted abductions of my girlfriend, Smith." The threat falls from my lips before I can stop it. I hadn't intended to let him know his man failed, but my brain didn't stop my knee-jerk reaction until it was too late. The cards are on the table before I intended to play them.

"Abduction?" His voice quips. "I don't know what you're talking about."

I scoff in disbelief. "Don't play dumb with me. You sent that goon to take Ginny."

"I assure you, Mr. Sterling, I have no knowledge of any attempted abduction."

"Bullshit," I hiss. "He told us he was paid to take her and keep her as an insurance policy, and whoever paid him needed to keep their mole in line. Sounds an awful lot like you, now doesn't it?"

Smith's sigh comes through the receiver. "I didn't order it, but it could have come from higher up."

"Get them to back off."

"You're in no place to issue demands, Mr. Sterling. Let me be clear… if you don't come through with my information soon, I won't be held responsible for any further actions taken to ensure its retrieval."

"Send someone else after Ginny, and the deal is off. Your leverage against me will be gone. Send another fucking person after her, and they'll find themselves visiting Death Valley. I've been told it's nice this time of year." The reveal of where they could find Roman slips too easily from my mouth. If he wanted information, I'd just given him something that would keep him busy for now. Death Valley is over five thousand square miles. If Roman is indeed a part of his operation, he'll no doubt want to find his body. The body that is now a needle in the desert haystack. "Do I make myself clear?"

"You have a week. Get me that information." The line goes dead, leaving me standing there in silence.

The steam from the shower is building up around me. How the hell am I supposed to crack this flash drive? It is like trying to solve a Chinese puzzle box. I can't get a handle on it. And with Smith breathing down my neck, the pressure is mounting.

I step into the shower, letting the hot water cascade over me. My mind is racing with possible solutions, but nothing comes to mind. It is like repeatedly hitting a wall.

Exiting the shower, I dry myself off and get dressed. My mind is still preoccupied with the flash drive when I return to the bed, where Ginny still sleeps soundly. I envy her ability to shut off the world around her and sleep.

Leaning down, I give her a light kiss on the forehead. She stirs lightly but doesn't wake. I could sit here for hours, watching her sleep, but I have work to do. I need to figure out how to crack this damn flash drive.

Kissing her one more time, I head to my closet and pull out the used laptop I purchased from a pawn shop after I found the flash drive. V's computers or any other club computers were out of the question. I'd gone so far as to buy a satellite internet dongle to stay off the club's Wi-Fi. The less I had connecting me to this, the better. The encryption software I had been running overnight is still on the screen—the green lines of code trailing along the prompt window.

I take it into the bathroom and close the door behind me so as not to wake Ginny.

I try to focus on the task at hand, but my mind is preoccupied with Smith's threat. It's not something to take lightly. Men in his position aren't known for being gentle. To hold that much authority in a government office means only one thing—he's fought his way to the top. If he tried to take her once, even if he denies it, he'll try again if I don't figure out this fucking flash drive.

I take a deep breath and focus on the screen before me. The encryption software has made some progress, but it's not enough. I need to find a way to break through the encryption. While I am not as good as V, I had taken several computer coding classes in college, despite my parents' protests about not focusing on business classes.

If they could only see me now—how disappointed they would be in their golden boy.

The heir who walked away from the money and their bullshit.

Not once have they tried to contact or find me.

They have what they want, my brother filled my shoes immediately. I'd seen he'd gotten married to another heiress. Hotels, I think. Good for him. He's living the life they wanted for me.

Refocusing, I type on the keyboard, trying different methods to break through the encryption. But it's like trying to break into a safe without the combination. I'm making some progress, but it's slow and tedious.

My fingers twitch over the keys, hesitant to click enter. I need to be careful—one wrong move and I could lose everything, but I am running out of time. I have to take a risk. I hit enter and watch as the screen transforms, lines of code flying across the screen in a blur. I sit in the bathroom for hours, listening for Ginny to stir or someone to move in V's room. Silence.

My fingers ache, my eyes are dry, but I keep going. I can't afford to stop. Finally, after what seems like an eternity, I see it. A single file on the flash drive lights up on the screen. I double-click it, my heart racing as I wait for it to open.

But nothing happens.

The file won't open. I have the information, but it's useless to me if I can't open it. Not without the password. Frustrated, I slam my fists down on the counter, cursing loudly. The bathroom echoes with my frustrations, but Ginny doesn't stir.

I take a deep breath and try to focus again. There has to be a way to find the password or crack open the file. But how? I feel like I've exhausted every option.

I stare at the screen for a few moments, my mind searching for anything that could help me.

And then it hits me.

I only have one choice.

Go back to the fucking source.

V.

I exit the bathroom.

Disconnecting the flash drive from my laptop, I shove it in my pocket and put my laptop back into the hiding space in my closet.

Going to V is a risk, but I'm getting nowhere fast. Outside of hiring another hacker and potentially handing out incriminating information to another party, it's the only option I have. The only thing is *how do I get him to help?* Handing him his flash drive and asking him to crack it would be a flashing sign over my head as the mole Roman mentioned.

There has to be a way. I just need to figure it out.

Checking on Ginny, she's still fast asleep in our bed. I grab my cut and head out of the room, leaving a note for her in case she wakes.

Heading into the common room, there are few new club girls working in the kitchen under Ruby's watchful eye. Ruby's been here since Raze took over the club after his dad died. While she moved more freely than the rest of the girls, she'd become more of a den mother to the ladies who stayed here.

The smell of a hot breakfast being prepared wafts into the common area.

I make my way to V's office. The hallway is empty, and I breathe a sigh of relief. As I enter his office, he looks up from his computer screen, slightly surprised to see me. "What are you doing here?" he asks, his eyebrows raised.

"I could ask you the same thing. Do you fucking sleep in here?"

V smirks. "Presley sent me out in the middle of the night for fucking In-N-Out. Couldn't go back to sleep, so I just came here. She snores like a fucking freight train when she's pregnant."

I stifle a laugh. After sharing a wall with him, I know for a fact he does too. It's ironic that his wife's snoring keeps him awake like his did me years ago. There was more than one occasion when I considered smothering his ass with a pillow to get some sleep.

"It's not funny. Between her and Han, the only time I get any sleep is when I'm here with my ladies." He reaches out and pats the computers in front of him. "They purr quietly."

"How you ended up with Presley, I'll never know."

"Trust me, I ask myself that question every fucking day." He pauses. "What brings you here?"

"Need to ask you a tech question," I admit.

"You? A tech question? Let me just get this out of the way. *Have you tried turning it off and on again?*" He smirks quoting from his favorite TV show *The IT Crowd.*

My lips thin. "Really, asshole?"

"What?" He shrugs. "It's an honest question."

V smiles but turns his head back to the monitors

above us as a motion sensor dings. He peers up at the monitor. In grainy black and white, I see his wife padding through the kitchen in their house with their son tucked around her hip.

"Is that Presley?"

V spins around in his chair with a serious look on his face. "You didn't see shit."

It hits me. He's rigged up cameras at their house. I knew he had them linked to the club monitors… but that's interesting. "Are you stalking your wife when you're here?"

"No," he blurts out.

"Oh shit. She doesn't know, does she? Does Raze?"

"Fuck no," V snaps, his expression darkening. "Nobody knows except for you. And I'd prefer it if you kept your mouth shut about it."

"Of course," I say, holding up my hands in defense. "But why the cameras?"

"I installed them for safety reasons," he says. "You never know who might come after your family. I'm surprised you haven't asked me to tag Ginny for you."

The idea hits me. After what had happened with Roman, I could have done that. I could have invaded her privacy and tagged her with a tracker to keep tabs on her. While I would never do it, V doesn't know that. This could work.

"That's why I popped by. This shit with Roman has me on edge. I know you helped put trackers on Ricca and Asher. I want something like that. Something discreet."

V's eyes widen, and there's a grin on his face.

"You came to the right person. How deep do you want to go?" He spins his chair to the left, pushing out of it and stalking over to one of his cabinets. He searches for a few minutes before pulling out a large box and setting it on the desk in front of him.

"Dude, is that all tracking devices?" I fire back.

"Yeah?"

I blink. There must be dozens of devices in there. He pulls out a few, each one smaller than the other.

I take one of the devices from him and examine it closely. It's so small, I could easily hide it unnoticed. "Is this just a tracker, or does it have audio and video?"

"Ah, not that one." He takes it from me, adds it back to the table, and selects a larger one on the top of his pile. "This one has audio and video."

It's small, no larger than a quarter. I nod my approval. "This should work. Can you show me how to use it?"

"Of course," he says, taking the device from me.

He begins to explain the process of attaching it to someone and setting up the tracking software on my phone. He helps me download the app and sync it to the camera. We test it out. V's face and the two of us talking show up clearly on my phone.

"Where the hell did you get this?"

"Don't ask. Don't tell."

I raise my eyebrows at V's answer, curious about where he got his hands on such advanced technology but knowing better than to push the subject any further.

I help him put the rest of his trackers back into the box. I accidentally knock one on the floor. He bends over to grab it, and I take my chance, slipping the flash drive from my pocket and letting it fall into the pile on the table. V stands back up, blowing on the tracker screen to clean it off.

"This yours?" I ask, showing him the flash drive in the pile.

He takes it from my outstretched hand, studying it. "Shit. I've been looking for this."

"What is it?" I ask, curious.

"Just some files I was working on," V replies, but I can see the tension in his shoulders. "They're from a project I'm working on for Raze."

I nod, not wanting to push him any further.

"Thanks for showing me how to use the tracker. I owe you one."

V nods, still studying the flash drive in his hand. "Yeah, you do."

"Keep this between us," I add. "You can imagine how badly hell would break loose if Ginny found out she was being tracked... Ratchet too. I think he's finally accepting my dating his sister, and the last thing I need is to piss him the fuck off again."

"I didn't give you shit." V smiles. "Because his ass would flay me alive for giving it to you."

I laugh, knowing full well that Ratchet has a protective streak a mile wide when it comes to his little sister.

"Thanks again, man."

"No problem." V waves me off before turning his attention back to the monitors hanging above us. "And if you need anything else, you know where to find me."

I nod and make my way out of V's office.

While he has the flash drive back in his possession, it's all going to plan. I may not be able to access the files, but he can. And after everyone leaves tonight, I'll be planting this tracker in his office.

I just have to find a way to live with the guilt.

Chapter 18

GINNY

LUCAS HAS BEEN DISTANT.

Even with my arms wrapped around his torso on the bike, he feels so far away. I feel Slider's muscles tense under my embrace as we drive toward Presley's new office for my weekly appointment. His attention is focused on the road ahead, but his mind is clearly somewhere else.

I can't help but wonder what's wrong. The uncertainty nags at me. I try not to let it show and keep my grip tight around him. Maybe it's his new role in the club keeping him quiet. Darcy had warned me that being with a biker came with secrets. Things they would never tell us, but this seems more than that—something bigger than only club secrets.

Presley's new office appears on the corner ahead of us. The newly remodeled Spanish Colonial Revival building stands out against the more modern offices flanking it. Lucas finds an open spot at the front of the building and backs in. He dismounts first before helping me off his bike.

"What time do you think you'll be done?" he asks flatly.

"Probably around four."

"Okay." His answer is curt, and I can see the tension in his jawline. "Text me if it'll be longer. I'll be back to get you." He kisses my temple. "Tell her I said hi."

I stand there, watching him as he walks back to his bike and leaves, turning the corner and disappearing from view.

For a moment, I'm alone, confused, battling with hurt. I hate this feeling of uncertainty and not knowing what's going on. But then I remember why I'm here—my weekly appointment with Presley. I take a deep breath and walk toward the office building, pushing Lucas' strange behavior to the back of my mind for now.

Presley is waiting for me in her new reception area, which looks more like an art gallery than a therapist's office. Large, colorful paintings hang on the walls, and a vase of fresh flowers sits on the coffee table. It is the exact opposite of her old office back in Kentucky.

I can't help but smile at the sight of it all. Presley has always been different in every way in her mannerisms, how she dresses, her choice of work, and her perspective on life—the exact opposite of her brother, Raze. Where he is hard and unwavering, she's soft and comforting. That's why I feel so comfortable talking to her about everything that's happened to me. She understands me, even in my most vulnerable moments.

"Hey! Come in," she greets and hugs me tightly. "You look good."

"Thanks," I say, feeling grateful for the compliment. Her swollen belly is more prominent than it had been last week. Her hands fall to it, gifting me a beaming smile.

"Where did that come from?"

"Out of nowhere. I woke up and bam, baby belly."

"Well, you look good."

"Tell that to my aching back. I'm only five months pregnant. I don't think I was this big with Han."

The mention of her toddler's name sends a ripple of amusement across my face. How V had convinced her to name their son after one of his favorite fandom characters, I will never know. Knowing V, if this baby is a girl, she'll be Leia or Ahsoka if he has his way.

"Come on in. We'll get started."

We walk into her spacious office. It's simple yet elegant. The walls are painted a soft beige with a mini fountain in the corner and an overstuffed chaise lounge at the center of the room. Presley takes her seat across from me, and I begin to feel at ease.

"So, tell me. What's new? How are you and Lucas doing?" she asks, leaning forward.

I try to act nonchalant, but my voice gives me away. "Honestly, things are a bit off. I can't put my finger on it. Something seems… wrong."

Presley is a master at reading emotions, and she easily catches what I'm saying. "What happened? Did he do anything? Say anything?"

"No, nothing like that… it's just that he's been distant lately. I can almost feel him slipping away, and I don't know why."

Presley takes a deep breath and looks at me thoughtfully. "Sometimes, people close off when they're dealing with something difficult. It's possible he's struggling with something and needs some time to process it on his own. He spent four years in prison, Ginny. It's not easy to survive that kind of life. I know you endured something similar, but for him, he may be fighting demons you don't know about. Has he talked much about his time there?"

"To be honest, he barely talks about anything. When it comes to our sex life, we connect. It's ethereal. But talking? It feels like I'm talking to a brick wall sometimes."

Presley nods in understanding. "It's not uncommon for people who have been through traumatic experiences to struggle with opening up. But, Ginny, communication is key in any relationship. You need to talk to him and let him know how you're feeling."

I already know that, but hearing it from Presley makes it feel like a concrete plan. I nod, realizing this is a possibility. "Do you have any advice on how I can help him?"

Presley smiles reassuringly. "Just keep being there for him, but also give him the space he needs."

"It's easy to say that than doing it, Presley. I don't know where to start. I want this to work for us and do this right. I just feel like I am losing him already."

Presley's expression turns softer, and she takes my hand. "Ginny, you have to trust that if the love between you is strong, it will find a way to work through any hardship. But it takes two people to make a relationship work. You can't carry the burden of his struggles on your own. You both need to put in the effort to stay connected and work through this together."

I nod, my eyes misting over with tears. Presley is right. Lucas and I need to work on our communication and rebuild the trust and connection we once had. But it won't be easy. We rushed so headlong into this that I don't think either of us looked past our physical connection to forge the emotional one.

"You two have been through so much together, and that connection won't just disappear. But if you're feeling anxious, have you considered talking to him about seeing a therapist together?"

"He'd never do that." I scoff. "Has V or any of the other guys come to see you?"

Presley gives me a knowing look before shaking her head. "You know I can't tell you that, but be patient with him."

"It's just hard when I feel like I am in the dark."

She looks me in the eyes before continuing, "I know, but remember that joy can be found in unlikely places. You'll find it," she assures me. "This life isn't always easy. Many women have thrown in the towel and given up, but if you two keep trying, the outcome will be nothing short of beautiful."

"I needed to hear that." More than her words, but the reassurance that Lucas and I had found each other despite all the odds. Four years away from each other couldn't stop our feelings. We can find a way around whatever is holding him back. "Thank you, Presley," I say, my voice thick with emotion.

"Anytime, Ginny," she responds with a gentle

smile. "And remember, you're not alone in this. You have me and the support of our other ladies. We've been in your shoes. Come to us when you need help."

The idea of taking my relationship to the other ladies builds a pit of uneasiness in my stomach. Sharing such an intimate part of me openly outside of Presley seems daunting, but maybe it's what I need.

We continue to talk for an hour, and when I leave, I feel lighter. As I step out of the building, Lucas is waiting for me on his bike.

"Hey," he says softly, holding out his hand for me. I take his hand and climb onto the back of the bike, feeling his tension ease under my touch. We ride silently for a few minutes, the wind whipping around us as the motorcycle speeds down the road. The tension between us is palpable, but I don't know how to break it. I'm scared that if I speak up, I'll say the wrong thing and make everything worse. But as we turn onto the street for the clubhouse, I decide to take a chance. He pulls into the parking lot and backs up his bike by the rear entrance. He kills the engine, helping me off the bike before he dismounts.

"Can we talk?"

He glances over his shoulder at me, his eyes guarded. "About what?"

"About us."

Lucas flinches. "I was worried you were going to say that."

"Things have been weird between us lately," I admit, my eyes cast down toward the ground as I speak. "You've barely said two words to me since our fight. You haven't touched me. What did I do wrong?"

"It's not you." His voice is rough and harsh.

"Then what is it? One minute, you can't keep your hands off of me. The next minute, it's like I don't exist. Is there someone else? Are you tired of me already?"

My words break through, and his eyes snap harshly to mine. "Don't you dare accuse me of stepping out on you, Gin. I'm not that kind of man."

"I don't think I know the man you are anymore." The truth punches me in the gut. "I know you've been through so much, but so have I. We're the only two people in this entire club who have been through hell and back like we have. I thought..." I trail off. "I thought that would help bind us together, but it feels like it's only dragging us further apart."

"I don't want to burden you with my problems, Ginny. You've been through so much already."

"Lucas, I'm your partner. Your problems are my problems. And I want to help you through them."

He looks at me for a long moment, his gaze searching. Then he leans forward and presses his lips to mine, his kiss desperate and hungry. I respond eagerly, feeling the familiar heat between us ignite. We pull apart, panting for breath, and he rests his forehead against mine.

"Ginny, I love you. I don't want to lose you," he says, his voice thick with emotion.

"I love you too, Lucas. But we can't keep avoiding the issues between us. We have to talk. What's going on?"

"Nothing is going on," he retorts immediately. He looks at me, his eyes full of uncertainty. "It's not that simple, Ginny."

"Make it that simple. Tell me what's going on so I can help you."

"I can't."

My heart drops at his words, the fear I've been pushing down for weeks now manifesting itself.

"Is it the club? Us? I feel like we've been spinning in circles for weeks now. I'm asking you to be honest. To let me in. We can work through anything as long as we face it together."

"Don't you think I want to tell you? If you only knew the consequences, baby, you wouldn't be asking me this."

I flinch. "Consequences? What consequences? What aren't you telling me?"

"Just drop it, okay? Leave it alone, and let me handle it."

I shake my head, feeling frustrated and weary. "No, that's not okay. You can't just shut me out and expect everything to be fine. We're a team, remember? We're in this together."

He sighs, his shoulders dropping. "I know. It's just… complicated. There are things I can't tell you."

"Is this about the club?"

"Drop it, Gin. You can't be a part of this."

"I won't judge you, Lucas. Whatever it is, we can get through this. Let me help you."

He looks at me for a long moment, his eyes searching mine. Then he takes a deep breath.

"No one can help me, Ginny. Not even you."

I watch Lucas walk away from me, his broad shoulders slumped, and hands shoved deep into his pockets. I know he's hurting and can feel the pain rolling off him in waves. But I don't know how to help him. I don't know what he's involved in or why he's so set on keeping me out of it. All I know is I can't stand to see him suffer.

"Lucas, please," I say softly. "You don't have to go through this alone."

He stops abruptly and turns to face me. In the

setting sunlight, I can see the lines of strain etched into his handsome face. He shakes his head, a rueful smile twisting his lips. "You have no idea what you're getting into, Gin."

"I don't care," I say fiercely. "I love you, and I won't let you push me away."

He stares at me for a long moment, his eyes flickering over my face as if searching for any sign of doubt. But there's only determination in my expression, a fierce resolve that matches his.

Finally, he sighs and steps closer to me, his hand cupping my cheek. "Maybe you should let me go. It would be better for both of us."

Chapter 19

SLIDER

FOR DAYS, I've watched the camera feed from V's office. Hours of footage of V working on his computer or playing some fucking underground video game while he waits on his computer to crack something. I'd even seen him watching *Star Wars* and reenacting part of the movie with one of his fucking dolls, only cementing that V is a fucking weird guy.

Watching the feeds has kept my mind off the fact that Ginny had been gone for three days. After our fight, she decided it was better for her to stay with her brother for a few days.

I'd tried to text her.

Nothing.

Calls unanswered.

I fucked up.

I knew that.

I'd let the pressure and stress from this situation with Smith invade my relationship with her. I know Ginny means well. I'd apparently done a shit job of hiding the churning storm brewing inside me from her. I want to shield her from this and the fallout that is barreling toward us. If I could save one person from this, it had to be her. She deserved that much.

I knew I should have apologized quicker or tried to do something to make it up to her, but maybe it was for the best. She's safer at Ratchet's.

The motion sensor on the camera app dings, dragging me back from my self-loathing and guilt about Ginny.

I see something different on the screen. V is at his desk, computers and monitors still bright in front of him, but someone else has walked in—a woman. A cloak covers her body, the hood hiding her face. V's torso fills the frame as he hugs her.

"Who the fuck is that?"

The camera angle is too low to make out her features.

The woman leans down, whispering into V's ear. I hear him chuckle. His hands fall to her hips before he drags her into his lap in his desk chair.

Aw. Fuck. This can't be happening.

The woman leans in, kissing V. Her naked thighs straddle his hips on either side of the chair he is sitting on, and her face is still obscured from view. V rips his shirt over his head, dragging the woman back to his lips. He shifts, his mouth on her neck.

I blink, unsure of what I am seeing. *Is V cheating on his pregnant wife?* He loves her, doesn't he? I watch until his hands go for her hood, drawing it back. Presley's face comes into clear view, along with the pointed ear prosthetics hidden under her cloak.

"Fuck, I love it when you dress up for me, baby," V coos before I slam the app shut.

"Oh, fuck no." My head is spinning. The image of Presley on V's lap, with his hands all over her, is burning into my mind. And the fact that Presley is wearing cosplay elf ears is simply too much. I can't believe what I've just seen. Clearly, his nerd shit is contagious. I should have known V isn't the type of guy to cheat on his wife, but I hadn't pegged Presley as someone who might enjoy cosplay and role play. I'm not the kind of guy to kink shame, but fuck, I didn't need to watch that shit.

As I sit staring at my phone, I feel a pang of guilt. Despite everything, Ginny is still the one I want to talk to about this. But she's gone, and I have no idea when she will be back. I know there is no point in trying to call her again. She hasn't answered any of my other calls. Why would this one be any different?

Instead, I lean back in my chair and close my

eyes. My mind is racing, trying to process everything that's happened in the last few days—Smith's threats, my fight with Ginny, and now this.

It's all becoming too much.

I need a drink.

I get up from my chair and make my way to the bar. I can still hear V's voice in my head, calling Presley 'baby' and telling her how much he loves it when she dresses up for him. It makes me sick to my stomach.

I pour myself a glass of whiskey and take a sip, relishing the burn as it goes down my throat. I need something to take my mind off of everything that's happening. I need to forget about Ginny, V, and Smith for a while.

As I sit there, nursing my drink, I realize that instead of calling or texting Ginny, I must find her and apologize. I rub my forehead, trying to think of a way to approach Ginny without further damaging our relationship.

"You look like you've seen some shit," Ruby remarks from behind the bar.

"You have no idea." I gulp a mouthful of whiskey and wince as it burns my throat.

"Ginny hasn't been around the last few days. She okay?"

"Wouldn't know."

Ruby looks at me with concern in her eyes. "Everything okay between you two?"

I shake my head, taking another sip of whiskey. "No, not really. We had a fight. She left to stay with her brother for a while."

"That would explain why she's been gone."

"Yeah," I mutter. "I fucked up, said some shit I shouldn't have, and she's cut me off. I don't know what to do without making it worse."

She leans in a little closer. "Seems to me you already know what you need to do." Ruby nods, looking thoughtful. "The first step is to find her."

"Easier said than done."

"If relationships were easy, I'd been in one, Slider." She smiles. "Trust me… go find her. Stop waiting for her to come to you. A woman like her wants to be chased, so show her you still want her."

"I doubt that will work."

I try to sound nonchalant, but my guilt is bubbling to the surface. I need to find Ginny and make things right between us. Ruby gives me a sympathetic look, and I can tell she understands what's going on. She's always been excellent at reading people.

"You gonna go talk to her?" she asks.

"Yeah. Yeah, I think I am."

I finish my drink and stand, my mind fixed on finding Ginny. I don't know where to start, but I'll figure it out. I thank Ruby and leave the bar, the hot summer air hitting me like a physical force. While Southern California doesn't have humidity, the dry heat is still hot.

I find my bike where I left it, straddle the seat, and rev the engine, the sound drowning out all other thoughts in my mind.

I need to find Ginny and make things right between us.

I push off, heading toward Ratchet's house.

The wind whips through my hair as I ride, my thoughts consumed by Ginny. The memory of how she looked at me—hurt and betrayed—still haunts me. I need to fix things before it's too late.

The ride is short, but my stomach coils in knots as soon as his house comes into view. I park out front— the spaces usually occupied by Ricca's SUV and Ratchet's bike are empty. I peer up at the house, and the blinds are drawn closed.

I hesitate before getting off my bike and approaching the front door. I knock, but there's no answer. I try again, this time knocking louder. Still, no response.

I start to panic. *Where could she be?* I pull out my cell and try calling her again, but it goes straight to voicemail. I leave a message, begging her to call me back.

With my hand hovering over the doorknob, I hesitate, the keypad taunting me. Ratchet had given me the code to his house in case of an emergency so I could enter without a second thought.

What if Ginny doesn't want to see me? What if I make things worse? But I can't leave things like this. I need to make it right.

With a deep breath, I punch in the code, turn the knob, and step inside. The air is still and quiet, the only noise coming from the humming of the ceiling fan. I call out Ginny's name, but there's no answer. My heart sinks. *Where could she be?*

I walk through the darkened living room, my eyes adjusting to the dim light. The door to the bedroom is partially open, and I push it open the rest of the way. *Empty.*

I try to keep the panic from rising as I move through the house, checking room after room, but she's nowhere to be found. I begin to second-guess myself.

Had she even come here?

Has she left entirely?

"This is fucking useless," I mutter to myself, angry that I hadn't come here sooner.

Suddenly, I hear a noise coming from the kitchen,

the backdoor opening with footsteps. I make my way back down the hallway.

I freeze in my tracks, my breath catching in my throat.

There, standing at the counter, is Ginny. Her back is to me. A few grocery sacks lay in front of her on the counter. She's wearing a white tank top and a flowy mid-knee skirt, her dark hair cascading down her back. I can't help but admire how beautiful she looks.

I stay in the doorway, not sure if I should approach her. I want to go to her and explain everything, but I'm scared of pushing her away even more.

Terrified I'm too late.

She turns, her eyes connecting with mine. She screams. "What the hell are you doing here? How did you get in?" she demands, her eyes flashing with anger and fear.

"I'm sorry. Ratchet gave me the code. I need to talk to you."

"We have nothing to talk about," she snaps, turns her back to me, and resumes unpacking groceries from the bags on the counter.

"Ginny, please. I know I messed up. I shouldn't have said those things. I'm sorry. I just want to make it right between us."

"You're damn right you messed up," she says, still not looking at me.

"I know. I was an idiot, but I want to fix it. Please, just hear me out." I move closer, reaching out to touch her arm, but she jerks away.

"Don't touch me!" she yells, finally turning to face me. "What do you want from me, Lucas? You showed me who you really are, and now you want me to forgive and forget? I can't do that."

"I know, and I don't expect you to. I only want to try and make it right. Can we talk?"

She lets out a heavy sigh, her eyes locked onto mine. I can see the hurt and anger swirling within them, but there's something else there too—a flicker of something that gives me hope.

"Fine. We'll talk."

An uncomfortable silence settles between us for a few moments, neither of us quite sure where to begin.

Finally, Ginny lets out a deep breath and turns to me. "Why did you say those things, Lucas? What did I ever do to make you think that way about me?"

"It wasn't about you," I blurt out. "It was about me and my insecurities. I took it out on you, and I'm so sorry."

"That's not good enough," she says, her voice

hardening. "You hurt me, Lucas. You made me feel like shit."

"I know, and I hate myself for it," I reply, my voice thick with emotion. "I'm sorry, Ginny. I really am. I said some things I didn't mean, and I hurt you. I love you, and I don't want to lose you. I know I don't deserve your forgiveness, but I'm willing to do whatever it takes to earn it."

She remains silent, her eyes fixed on mine. I know she's considering my words.

"I'll do anything, Ginny. Anything to make things right between us," I say, my voice cracking with emotion.

She sighs, a small smile tugging at the corners of her lips. "You're lucky I love you," she says, stepping closer.

Relief floods through me, and I wrap my arms around her, pulling her close. She hesitates for a moment before returning my embrace, and I can feel the tension melting away.

"I'm sorry," I whisper into her hair.

"I know," she says, her voice muffled against my chest. "And I forgive you. But we still have a lot to work through."

"I'll do whatever it takes," I promise, holding her tight.

We stand like that for a long moment, the only

sound the beating of our hearts. I lean down, kissing her. Her lips are soft against mine, and I feel the tension and hurt rolling off her in waves. But as we kiss, I can feel the anger and sadness start to disappear.

We pull back, our eyes locked onto each other's.

"We'll figure it out," she says with a slight smile.

"I know we will," I reply, my smile matching hers. She responds with a passionate kiss, her hands sliding up to grip the back of my neck. I deepen the kiss, pouring all my love and remorse into it.

We pull away, breathless and panting.

Ginny looks up at me, a fire in her eyes I haven't seen in a long time. "I have an idea," she says, a mischievous grin on her lips. "How about we make up for lost time? Just you and me, here in this kitchen."

My heart races as I realize what she's suggesting. "Are you sure?"

"I've never been more sure of anything," she replies, a wicked gleam in her eyes.

I take her hand, leading her to the nearby counter. I grip her hips, lifting her. Her legs wrap around my waist.

We share another passionate and hungry kiss. I slide my hands up her thighs and under her skirt, feeling the heat of her skin against my palms. She moans into my mouth, and I know she's just as desperate for this as I am.

I lower her onto the counter, our lips still locked together. Her hands slide up under my shirt, her nails digging into the skin of my back. I feel the fire inside her, burning hot and bright.

"You're soaked, Gin."

She nods silently.

My fingers trace her delicate skin before I slide a finger inside her. Her back arches, a moan escapes from her lips, and the walls of her cunt clench around me.

"Yes..." She gasps, her head falling backward. "Fuck me," she demands.

Her hands fall to my jeans, fumbling with the button and zipper while my fingers are still deep inside her. She shoves them down low on my hips, my hard cock springing free. Her hands then go to her panties, pushing my hand away from her drenched pussy, before tugging them down her bare legs and kicking them onto the floor at my feet.

With one movement, I'm inside her.

Ginny breathes in sharply, her nails digging into my arms. I start thrusting, her breathing speeds up, and I feel her walls tighten around me.

"Oh, Lucas..." She moans, her body quivering against mine. "Yes, yes, *yes*."

"Say my real name, Gin. Tell me whose fucking your pussy. Who owns it."

"You do," she moans.

"Say it," I demand.

"You own my pussy, Lucas."

"That's right, baby. This pussy is mine. Mine to lick. Mine to fuck. *Mine*."

I continue to tease and pleasure her, taking her higher and higher until she is perfectly perched on the edge of a sweet release. Her body trembles beneath mine, and she gasps my name, pushing me deeper.

Her walls tighten around me, her warmth inviting me home.

We move in unison, our movements, a dance that only we know. Our moans meld together, creating a chorus of beautiful, orgasmic sounds.

My hips buck wildly against hers, her head is thrown back in pleasure, and our moans fill the kitchen. I feel my climax building, and I know she's close.

Our eyes lock as I move faster and faster. Her body quivers around me as she cries out my name one last time, and her orgasm rips through her before mine tears through me.

We stay still and silent until we both come down from our high.

I pull away from her, a smile stretching from ear to ear. "Well," I say, my voice gruff. "That was one way of making up for lost time."

"It certainly fucking was," a voice answers back from behind us.

Ginny peers over my shoulder, a look of shock on her face.

"Tell me that's not your brother." I groan, dropping my head.

It is.

The asshole's standing in the doorway with a murderous look on his face.

Chapter 20

GINNY

TALKING my brother off the murderous ledge after catching Lucas and me in his kitchen had been a bigger deal than I had expected. Jude was livid—still is. He could barely look at me when he'd come by the clubhouse, and the looks he gave Lucas, *phew*. I knew Jude had always been fiercely protective, but I had never seen him like this before. I tried apologizing, explaining that it just happened, but he wouldn't listen. The only thing I have left now is let him cool off and hope Ricca can talk some sense into him.

"Can we go somewhere today?"

Lucas peers up from his cell. "What?" He's been glued to it for days. He locks the screen, shoving it into his pocket.

"Let's get out of here."

"Why?" he asks.

"I don't know. I feel like escaping for a bit… just the two of us." I can tell he's not really interested in going somewhere, but I persist. "Please?"

Lucas sighs and nods. "Yeah, sure. Where do you want to go?"

I think for a moment before answering, "Let's go to the beach."

He raises an eyebrow. "The beach? It's like the surface of the fucking sun outside. It's gonna be packed."

"I know," I say, smiling. "But sometimes it's nice to be somewhere completely different from here. I'll pack a bikini." I waggle my eyebrows, hoping the temptation will entice him enough to agree to my idea. "What about Venice Beach?"

"Do you want me to commit murder today, Gin?"

"What?" I feign ignorance.

"You want me to take you to Venice Beach, where all the fucking meatheads workout while you're wearing a bikini?"

I laugh. "Well, when you put it that way, it doesn't sound like the best idea ever."

"Exactly." Lucas looks relieved.

"But seriously, Lucas, I need to get away from the clubhouse for a while. Everything's so tense after what happened with Jude. I need a break."

There's a moment of silence between us. I'm not

sure if Lucas is going to agree with me or not, but then he nods slowly. "All right. Let's go to the beach."

We pack our bags and head out. The ride is long and hot, the sun beating down on us, but it's worth it when we finally see the ocean stretching out before us. The beach is crowded like Lucas had predicted, but we find a spot near the water's edge and lay down our towels.

As I'm taking off my sundress, I feel Lucas' eyes on me. The black string bikini I'd chosen to wear barely covers anything. I smile, watching his mouth clench. I purposely spin, putting my ass toward him as I kneel to straighten out my towel.

"Goddammit, Gin."

"What?" I coyly smile.

"You know exactly what you're doing," he grumbles, a hint of a smile playing on his lips.

"Do I?" I reply playfully.

He rolls his eyes, but the tension seems to ease out of him. "You're trying to kill me."

"I'm not trying to kill you." I chuckle.

"I'm not complaining," he says. "But now I can't take my eyes off you. First asshole that looks your way is losing their eyes."

"Stop being dramatic. No one is going to look this way with you sitting over there brooding away." I laugh and settle onto my towel, enjoying the feeling of the sun on my skin.

"I'm not being dramatic," he grumbles. "I don't like anyone staring at what's mine."

I laugh again, but I feel warmth fill my heart. I love how Lucas can be so possessive of me even when I'm in the wrong. It gives me the feeling of being safe and loved.

"Now, can we just relax and have a good time?" I ask.

"Fine!" He scoffs.

Lucas lays down next to me, his eyes closed. We lay in silence, the only sounds around us are the crashing of the waves and the chatter of the people nearby.

"What was it like for you in prison?" I ask. The question has been swirling in my mind since he came back. He hasn't mentioned his time once, and his letters revealed nothing.

Lucas takes a deep breath before answering, "It was hell, Gin. But I don't want to talk about it."

I turn my head to look at him, my heart heavy with the weight of his pain. "I understand," I say softly.

"No, you don't." He shakes his head. "You have no idea what it's like being in a cell all day, every day. Not knowing when you'll get out. The food was shit, the guards were assholes, and the inmates were worse."

I reach out and take his hand, lacing our fingers together. "I'm sorry," I say quietly.

"Do you want to know the worst part? I had no idea where you were or if you were okay. I didn't even find out you were out of protective custody until six months after the fact. No one told me anything."

The revelation shocks me. "No one told you?"

"Not a fucking soul. The week I got your letters, Raze had been to see me. You'd been back five months, and the bastard didn't have the decency to tell me."

He doesn't say anything for a long time. We just lay there, holding hands in silence. The sun beats down on us, but it doesn't feel as hot anymore—the ocean breeze cutting the temperature down enough to make it less uncomfortable.

"I don't understand why they didn't tell you. I tried to come see you, but they wouldn't let me."

Lucas sits up on his elbows, unlacing our hands. "They wouldn't let you come see me?"

"No." I shake my head. "I thought you didn't want to see me. It wasn't until I got your letters when I came back home that I knew you had even thought about me."

My brother gave me the letters as a Christmas present. I'd lost count of how many times I'd reread them, savoring every word. If I couldn't see or touch him, they were the next best thing and my way of continuing to feed our connection despite being so far away.

"I thought about you every day, Gin. You were what got me through the nights." He looks over to me. "I kept fighting for the next day because of you."

A tear escapes my eye and slides down my cheek. "I'm sorry I wasn't there for you," I whisper.

"You were there, Gin. You were in my heart, and I knew I could survive anything as long as I had you." He reaches out and wipes away the tear with his thumb before leaning in to kiss me gently.

"Was it the same for you?"

"Yes and no," I admit. "I was away from everyone, but I had Jude. When they took me back into custody, we'd negotiated a weekly call. It helped to talk to him, but I really wanted it to be you on the other end of the line."

Lucas reaches out and takes my hands, bringing them to his lips. "I'm so sorry, Gin. I wish I would have been there for you."

"I know," I say softly. "All of that time is behind us now. Rigo and his family are in jail. You served your sentence. We can finally live."

His face falls before he recovers.

"What was that look?"

"It's nothing," he answers. "It's hard to imagine a future right now. I'm still trying to get used to the fact I get to wake up next to you every day and not the image of you I had in my head."

"I understand. It must be hard to readjust after everything you've been through."

"It is, but I'm willing to do whatever it takes to make it work. I want to be with you, Gin," Lucas says, his eyes locking onto mine.

"I want that too."

Lucas reclines onto his towel, his eyes closed once again. I lay my head on his chest, listening to the rhythm of his breathing. The tension from the clubhouse feels miles away, and in this moment, it's just us.

I realize that Lucas is my safe place, and I am his.

We are each other's calm in a world that can be so chaotic.

I breathe in the salty air, content with the knowledge we will always have each other.

The sound of the waves lulls me asleep, and my eyes close until Lucas nudges me with his hand.

"Wake up, baby."

I sit up and stretch, blinking the sleep away. "What time is it?"

Lucas points up at the sky. "It's almost sunset. We better get packed and head back. It'll start getting cold soon."

I take one last look at the ocean before us, the sky painted a deep orange and pink, while he gathers up the towels and shakes off the sand. We both redress and head back to the parking lot.

"Thanks for dragging me out here."

I smile at him, feeling content. "I think we both needed today."

I help him stuff the towels into his saddle bags when I note his phone is vibrating in his pocket.

"I think someone's calling you."

He reaches down, retrieves his phone, and draws it to his ear.

"Yeah?" The person on the other end talks. Their words are mumbled enough with the sound of the ocean and the breeze that I can't make out what they're saying.

"Yeah, man. We're headed back down. Give us an hour."

He shoves his phone back into his pocket. "Everything okay?"

Lucas' face is grim. "Raze called a meeting."

My stomach knots and the peace we've had for the day is unraveling.

"What kind of meeting?"

"I'm not entirely sure yet. Raze's voice was cryptic, as always. But I have a feeling it's not good."

Lucas swings his leg over the bike and starts the engine. I climb on behind him, my arms wrapping around his waist. The bike's roar drowns out any other sound, and we speed down the road toward the clubhouse.

The parking lot is full of bikes when we arrive.

It's a full house, and full houses with this club is never a good sign.

Chapter 21

SLIDER

"SURPRISE!" the crowd yells as Ginny leads me into the common room.

"What the hell is this?"

"Your patch party." Ginny smiles up at me. "I know you said you didn't want one, but my brother told me this is a rite of passage. I didn't want you to miss out on something that seems pretty important."

"Is this why you wanted to suddenly go to the beach today?"

"It might have been," she answers coyly. "I mean, I did want to spend the day with you, but I also kind of needed you out of the clubhouse for this."

She waves to the common room. The entire club and their families are here. Kids of various ages dart around, and their shrill squeals are louder than the music or the crowd.

"Please don't be mad that we did this."

"I'm not mad."

V walks over with two beer bottles in his hands. He hands me one, clinking the neck to mine.

"May not have strippers or twins, but we have beer and our old ladies… so still a win in my book." Presley joins him, her hand on her swollen belly. "Congratulations!"

"Uh… thanks." The visual of what I had accidentally seen on the camera feed in his office flashes in my mind.

Their little boy, Han, toddles up next to Presley. She bends down to pick him up. "Drink?" he says, his hand outstretched to the beer in V's hand. He jerks it out of his grasp, correcting him.

"Not until you're sixteen and your mom is away."

Presley shoots him a glare. "What?"

"You know what."

"Fine. Not until you're eighteen."

Han begins to wiggle in her arms. "Down!"

I take a sip of the beer before setting it on a nearby table. The party is in full swing, and the clubhouse is packed with people. Irons, Tyson, Thrasher, and Thor are huddled in a corner, playing cards and smoking cigars. Dani and Darcy are dancing on the makeshift dance floor, swaying to the music with the kids. Raze's teenage son sits on the couch with a video game in his hand.

"Looks like Ky found your Switch, V."

"Son of a bitch, I thought I hid that better after the last time he grabbed it and beat my high score." V stalks off toward the boy with Presley hot on his heels.

We both head to the bar. Ginny orders a cocktail while I sip on the beer V had given me. The pink liquid sloshes over the sides of the glass as Ruby sets it on the counter.

"What is that?" I ask her over the sound of the music and laughter.

"Sex on the Beach." She winks.

Who the hell comes up with the names for these drinks? V had once tried to get me to try some shot called the Slippery Nipple or Slippery Dick or something like that. It looked like someone jizzed in a shot glass and added some liquid over the top of it. No fucking thank you.

Ginny sips her drink. Her hips sway to the music as her perfect lips engulf the tiny straw. As much as I didn't want a patch party, I have to admit I don't hate this. The escape from Smith is a welcome diversion today.

Ginny downs her drink, placing the empty glass

on the counter, then tugs at my arm, pulling me toward a group of people. "Come on, let's dance."

The music fills the room as we join the dancing group. Ginny moves her body against mine, her hips swaying in rhythm with the beat. Her hands rest on my shoulders as mine find her waist. I can feel her breath on my ear as she whispers, "You know, I've always had a thing for guys in leather."

"That so?"

"Mm-hmm."

I lean in closer, my lips brushing against her neck. "Well, lucky for you, I happen to be wearing some leather right now."

She giggles and pulls away, twirling around and dancing with the others. As I watch her, I can't help but feel grateful for her presence in my life. I chuckle before leaning down to capture her lips with mine. The kiss is heated, our tongues tangling together in a dance of their own. Suddenly, the room fades away, and all I can feel is her body pressed against mine—it feels like a damn sin made for a sinner like me.

"Stop fucking my sister on the damn dance floor," Ratchet mutters as he passes us. Ginny's smile fades into a frown.

"Ignore him, baby."

Ginny's eyes don't leave her brother's back as he walks away from us. The hurt is evident on her beautiful face. Sooner or later, we'll have to deal with what happened, but that won't be tonight.

"Let's get out of here."

She nods, my hand tightly gripping hers as we weave through the crowd. We exit the building and head toward her car, our fingers intertwined. I can feel the adrenaline coursing through my veins as we approach her vehicle. She presses her body against mine, her lips hot against my neck.

"I want you, now," she whispers.

Without another word, I lift her and press her against the car door. Her legs wrap around my waist as I grind against her, the heat between us igniting like wildfire. I run my hands down her body, cupping her ass and pulling her closer. Our lips meet again, more fervent than before.

"I need you," she moans against my lips.

I don't hesitate. I rip off her dress and the tiny bikini top, lower my head, and take her nipple into my mouth. She arches against me, her hands tangling in my hair. With a growl, I move my hand down to her bikini bottoms and rip them off. She shivers against the chilly night air, the moonlight high-lighting her beautiful body underneath its beams.

"I want to taste you." Ginny pushes me back, shifting away from the car door before switching places with me. Ginny falls to her knees, her hands greedily going to my jeans, freeing my cock from its restraints. She takes me into her warm mouth.

"Fuck, Gin." I hiss at the sensation. I groan the second her wet mouth takes me inside. My words come out as a guttural moan. She moans around me, and I can feel the vibrations down to my toes. Her tongue circles the head of my cock before she sucks me in deeper.

My shaft throbs between her lips as she slides her tongue along the bottom of it, then tugs upward to form a ring around the head when she finds it. My fingers grip her hair tightly as I thrust into her mouth, deepening my stroke down her throat.

I lean against the car, my head resting against the top as I moan and try to keep control. She moves her hands up and down my shaft as she takes me in and out of her mouth, the sensation overwhelming me in the best way possible. I start to speed up, my hands fisting in her hair as she takes me deeper and deeper. My body begins to tense, the sensation growing, begging me to succumb to it.

"Gin, I'm going to..." I shout, my whole body tensing.

Her hands cup my ass, pulling me closer to her as I let my pleasure fill her mouth, milking every drop from my cock. She looks up, licking my cum from her swollen lips.

I could come again at the sight.

Ginny looks up at me through her lashes before smiling around me. I can feel her drinking me in, her entire body quivering with pleasure. I can't stand it— I want more of her.

I pick her up and carry her to the other side of the car, pushing her against the hood and propelling her back toward me. I settle between her legs, pushing in deep.

"So ready for me, baby. Have you been thinking about this?"

"Yes." She nods. I pump into her harder and reach up to squeeze her breasts as I thrust into her, taking her pebbled nipples between my fingers.

"I need more," she begs.

She leans forward, pressing that gorgeous ass against me. My hands reach for her hair, creating a ponytail in my fist. Her head snaps back as I use it for leverage to thrust into her deeper. Ginny's body begins to clench around mine. I know she's close, but I am by no means done with her.

"Shit." She hisses, drawing my attention from her body to where she's looking. Someone steps outside. The red glow of a lit cigarette is the only thing we can see in the darkness around us.

Ginny's eyes widen. "What do we do?"

"Nothing," I answer, releasing my hold on her hair. It falls in thick waves down her back.

"But what if they hear or see us?"

"I don't give a damn, Gin. Nothing will stop me from using your perfect body," I whisper into her ear. "Let them see."

Ginny's entire body shivers beneath me. Her hands twist in the fabric of my shirt, her face turning bright red with embarrassment.

A voice comes from the direction of the clubhouse. "You hear something?"

Ginny looks up at me fearfully, her heart pounding wildly in her chest. I can see the fear radiating from her body, but I don't care. I'm not about to let some random person stop me from pleasuring the woman I love. She tenses underneath me, but I don't stop.

I grasp her hips and pound into her, the rhythm of pleasure rocking through her body and car. I'm pushing her closer and closer to the edge of completion. The air around us thickens with desire, and I can feel my orgasm building again.

"Say my name," I command between clenched teeth. "Say it, baby. Let them know who's fucking this pussy for anyone to see."

"Lucas!" she cries out as her whole body trembles

with pleasure, and I give into my desire, spilling my cum deep inside her.

The voice from before comes again. "I know you heard that."

"Must have been cats," he says, laughing.

"Cats don't say names, jackass."

We both laugh, knowing that neither of us could have been quiet enough for it to be mistaken for a cat. I pull out and help her back into her dress. I tuck myself back into my jeans, waiting for the two people outside to head back in.

"Ready to go inside?"

"Yeah, we probably should. It's probably rude to skip out on your own party… *twice*."

She presses her lips against mine, her embrace sending electricity through my veins. Her hand reaches down and grabs mine, intertwining our fingers as we walk back toward the clubhouse.

For the second time that night, Ginny made me feel alive. And I wasn't about to let anyone or anything get in the way of that.

Not even damn Smith.

Chapter 22

THE MORNING AFTER LUCAS' party, I wake with a splitting headache. My headache makes a new friend the next day as dizziness wrecks me. By the third day, my stomach decides to join the party, waking me up in the middle of the night to empty my gut. Lucas immediately woke, taking care to hold my hair as I wretched into the toilet for hours on end until there was nothing left inside me.

As the fourth day begins, I find myself weak and barely able to move out of bed, Lucas having to carry me to the bathroom when my feet give way from the dizziness. He's taken up a bedside vigil next to my side of the bed.

"I need to get up," I warn him.

Lucas' concern is growing graver as I try to sit up on the side of the bed, only for the world to start spinning as soon as I do. I press my hand against my head as if I could stop the motion that way.

"Are you dizzy again?"

I nod. The motion makes the spinning worse.

"It would make me feel better if you let Doc check you out, Gin. This is more than a hangover. It's been four days."

"I'm fine." I wave him off. "I must have picked up a bug. I just need to rest."

Lucas stands from his seat and approaches me with a worried look on his face. As he draws closer to the bed, he takes my hand and squeezes it tightly. "Please, Gin, for me. Let me call Doc to come take a look at you. I can't bear to see you like this anymore."

I look deep into his pleading eyes and take a deep breath before saying, "I'm sick, Lucas, not dying. It's just a bug. I probably got it from one of the kids at the party."

"No one else is sick, baby. Not even the kids. I checked."

"I'm telling you I am," I argue.

Lucas narrows his eyes, examining me closely. "It's not a bug, Gin. It's been four days, and you're only getting worse."

"Okay, okay. You win. Call Doc if it makes you

feel better, but don't be surprised when he says it's the flu like I told you."

Relieved, Lucas rushes to his cell and makes the call while I lay there feeling weak and helpless. Once he's done, he carries me to the bathroom and back to bed once I'm finished. The exhaustion of just the simple act of peeing is nearly too much for me.

Maybe he's right.

Maybe something is wrong.

Doc, the club's on-call physician, appears an hour later. His gray hair pokes through the door after he knocks. Lucas lets him in, ushering him to my bedside.

Doc takes one look at me and shakes his head. "How long have you felt like this?"

"Four days," he answers for me. "It started with a headache and has progressed to this. She's so dizzy I have to carry her to the bathroom."

Doc nods, a serious expression etched on his face.

"Let's see what's going on, shall we?" Doc pulls out his stethoscope and begins his examination. He listens to my heart and lungs before taking my temperature and checking my throat. I wince as he presses on my stomach.

"Does it hurt when I press here?" He shifts his large hands lower on my stomach. The pain makes me wince as he does. "Interesting," he mutters to himself before turning to Lucas. "I need to speak to Ginny privately if you don't mind."

"Of course," Slider murmurs, squeezing my hand before leaving the room. "I'll go get you some fresh water and ice chips."

I watch him go, a sense of dread creeping up my spine. What if it's something serious? What if I'm dying? The thought makes my stomach lurch, and I close my eyes, willing the nausea away.

"Ginny," Doc's voice brings me back to the present. "I'm going to ask you a few questions, okay? I need you to be honest with me."

I nod, my throat dry. "Okay."

"Have you had unprotected sex recently?"

My cheeks burn, embarrassment flooding through me. "No," I whisper. "I'm on the birth control injection. I'm not due for a new one for a few more weeks."

"When was your last period?"

I blink, unsure of what today even is. "It's on my phone." I point to it, and Doc hands it to me. I pull up my health app and find my period tracker. "Six weeks ago." *Panic sets in.* "I'm not pregnant, am I?"

"How long have you been taking your shots?"

"This would be the third or fourth one, I think. I started getting them when I came back in December."

"It's not uncommon for you to miss periods or to stop having them altogether with your method of birth control. In fact, most women stop having periods after a year on the shot. As long as you've been taking them on schedule, the likelihood that you're pregnant is statistically low. But just to rule things out, we'll do some blood work. I'll send the results to the lab, and we'll know for sure."

I let out a relieved sigh as Doc prepares the needle. The last thing Lucas and I need right now is an unexpected pregnancy. The idea of having a child scares me, especially now when I can barely take care of myself.

As the needle pierces my skin and Doc begins to draw my blood out, a knock comes on the door.

Lucas pokes his head in. "Is it all right if I come in?"

"Yes, yes," Doc mutters. His attention is on the needle in my arm and the little tubes of blood he's collecting. Lucas joins us, setting a fresh glass of water and ice chips next to me on the bedside table.

Doc takes the last tube of blood, adding it to the pile on the bed by my hip. He withdraws the needle and places a square of gauze on it, bending my arm at the elbow to apply pressure before eventually securing it with a bandage.

"What's the diagnosis?" Lucas asks.

"This is not the flu, and it's not some simple bug. You may have picked up a virus or a bacterial infection, or it may be something else entirely. I can't be sure at this point, but we need to figure it out."

I feel a knot of fear form in my stomach. This is not what I wanted to hear. I just want to go back to bed and sleep until I feel better, but I know that Lucas is right. This is not normal.

"Okay," I say, my voice feeling weak. "What do we need to do?"

"Let's see what the bloodwork says. I'll take it directly to the lab at my office with a *rush* order. We should know in a couple of hours if it's a simple infection or if it's something more serious that will require a trip to the hospital. In the meantime, stay in bed and off your feet as much as you can."

Doc rattles off a list of tests and procedures, a blur of medical jargon I can barely understand. Lucas listens carefully, nodding along. He looks so concerned and serious that I feel a flicker of gratitude. At least I have him by my side.

"You'll be okay, baby," he says, taking my hand.

I try to smile at him, but it comes out as a grimace. I feel so sick, tired, and helpless. I just want it all to be over. I want to feel better.

As the door closes behind Doc, Lucas turns to me.

"Whatever it is, we'll get through it. I'll be here for you every step of the way."

I nod weakly, grateful for his reassurance, but deep down, I'm terrified. *What if it's something serious? What if I won't get better? What if...* No. I can't think like that. Not until we know for sure.

While we wait for the lab results, time seems to move at a snail's pace. Lucas stays by my side, holding my hand and offering words of comfort. My mind races with thoughts and fears, wondering what will happen if it's something serious. Will I be able to fight it? Will I survive? The unknowns are almost too much to bear.

Despite my mind racing, I doze off and on until the sound of my cell brings me out of my sleep. I peer over, Lucas' spot empty. Reaching for my phone, I draw it to my ear.

"Hello?"

"Hey, Ginny, It's Doc. Your blood work results just landed on my desk."

My heart starts pounding in my chest. This is it, the moment of truth. "Okay, what does it say?" I ask, trying not to let my voice shake.

"You have a bacterial infection."

Relief washes over me. "We can treat that with antibiotics, right?"

"You certainly can. I've already called in a

prescription to the pharmacy the club uses. It should be ready in about an hour."

"At least I know why I feel so crummy," I admit.

"It might not just be the infection, Ginny. There's another result I think you may want to know about. You're pregnant."

My heart stops. The room starts to spin around me as I try to process what Doc just said.

Pregnant?

How can that be?

I can't be pregnant.

This can't be happening.

"Did you hear me, Ginny?" Doc's voice brings me back. "You're pregnant."

I take a deep breath, trying to steady my nerves. "Yes, I heard you. But how is that possible? I mean, I've been on the shot. I thought it was supposed to prevent pregnancy."

"It's not one hundred percent effective, Ginny," Doc explains. "There's always a chance of pregnancy, even on birth control."

I feel a wave of panic wash over me. I'm not ready for this. I barely know how to care for myself, let alone a baby. And what about Lucas? How will he react to the news?

"What do I do now?" I ask, my voice barely above a whisper.

"That's up to you, Ginny, but I recommend considering your options and talking to Lucas about it. It's important to make a decision soon. The longer you wait, the more complicated things can become."

I nod, even though he can't see me. "If you want to proceed with the pregnancy, I'll schedule you with the OBGYN in my practice for a prenatal visit to make sure everything is okay with the baby. And, of course, you need to start taking prenatal vitamins." He pauses. "If you don't, we'll discuss your options."

The words make my head spin.

Holy shit! I can't believe this is happening.

Chapter 23

SLIDER

"YOU NEED ANYTHING?" I ask Ginny as I help her onto the couch in the common room. Nearly a week after she'd fallen ill, she finally feels well enough to venture outside our room. Her stomach is still giving her fits, but she's been able to keep some food down, which is a vast improvement on where she was before she took the antibiotics Doc had prescribed.

"I'm okay."

"I've got her," Darcy remarks, joining her on the couch. "You don't want to be late. Michael was in a foul mood this morning when we left to come here. I'd hate for him to take it out on you for being late."

With a nod of thanks, I kiss Ginny on the top of her head and pivot toward the meeting room. It is full, and the noise of my club members talking over one another is deafening when I enter. I watch as they talk animatedly amongst each other. One of them spots me and nudges the others to indicate my presence.

"Good, we are all here. Let's begin," Raze says over the noise. We all fall to our usual seats around the table. Raze sits at the head with Hero and Ratchet flanking his sides. I settle in next to Ratchet, who doesn't look my way. Clearly, he's still angry with me about the incident in the kitchen with Ginny.

"V," Raze demands. "Put it up on the screen."

A video screen slides down from behind Raze, who shifts to the left to give us a clear view. V presses a key on his iPad, and a video pops up on the screen.

"Breaking News tonight from Inyo County. Park Rangers at Death Valley National Park reported that a body was discovered in the park. The deceased was found by local tourists hiking in the early morning hours." The newscaster's voice fills the room, and everyone goes quiet.

Ratchet peers over at me. I try to avoid his gaze, fixating on the screen and hoping to lessen the tension between us.

The newscaster continues, "The body was identified as Roman Ward, a thirty-five-year-old man from Seattle. Sources say the cause of death has not yet been determined, but park rangers are investigating it as a possible homicide. Anyone with information is urged to contact the authorities immediately. We'll continue to update you as more information becomes available."

The room falls silent as we all take in the news.

"This could be a problem," Hero says, breaking the silence.

"No shit," Thor scoffs.

"That's just the half of it. V?"

The video disappears from the screen, and a dossier with Roman's photograph pops up behind him.

"Our boy Roman wasn't a gun for hire. He was a fucking Fed, Homeland fucking Security according to the employment records I pulled from their database."

The room erupts into chaos as everyone starts talking at once, trying to understand what this means for us. I steal a glance at Ratchet, and he looks equally stunned.

I had a feeling he was running with Smith, but the confirmation hits me hard. Smith seemed genuinely unaware of the attempt to abduct Ginny, which means only two things—he was in on it and lied, or someone above him didn't like the progress and wanted to provide me with an incentive to work harder. Either way, I'm fucked.

"Well, this is fucking fantastic," Thor adds. "Where the fuck did you put him? Right in the middle of the park with a fucking balloon and flashing lights."

"He was well hidden," Ratchet fires back. "There's no way anyone could have found that body." He glances over at me. He's not wrong. We'd taken him far back into the park using a private access road that had been closed for years. Ratchet took great care to conceal his identity by pulling his teeth, taking his fingers, and burning the body. The smell of that bastard's flaming corpse had stuck in my nostrils since that night. The fingers had been tossed out the window over one of the rivers on our way out of the park. Finger fish food.

"It's true. The only thing left of him was fucking charred remains."

"If that's the case, how did they identify him?"

"The fuck if we know," Ratchet growls. "Are you trying to insinuate we have something to do with this?"

"He did say we have a rat. Seems pretty convenient he was found, and the only two people who knew where he was are sitting right across from me."

I can feel the tension in the room as Ratchet's words hang in the air. It's clear that everyone is on edge, and accusations are not going to make the situation any better.

I clear my throat before speaking, "Let's just take a step back for a second," I say firmly. "If Roman was indeed a federal agent, then we're dealing with an entirely different ball game here. The last thing we want is to be on their radar and at each other's throats."

Ratchet nods, and I can see the anger in his eyes start to dissipate. "Fine," he says. "What do you suggest we do?"

"Well, for starters, we need to find out more about the investigation. Who is in charge of it, what leads do they have… that kind of shit."

"We need to make sure our tracks are covered. If there's any evidence that could be linked back to us, we need to get rid of it," Hero adds.

More than they can ever know. If there's anything linking us to his death, Smith won't need the information from me about Mexico. It will give them the ammunition to come charging in here with a warrant. They won't need me at all.

"What I don't understand is his orders to take Ginny?" Thor remarks. "What's her role in this?"

"The only thing that makes sense is the Zezzas. Could they have the government in their pocket?"

The Zezzas and me.

"As big as they were before Ginny put Rigo and his associates away, it's a possibility," V admits. "A real fucking possibility."

I feel Ratchet's gaze burning into me, and I shift uncomfortably in my seat. "I don't know," I say honestly. "But we can't rule anything out at this point. We have to assume that every move we make is being watched and act accordingly."

Raze leans forward, his eyes flicking from me to Ratchet. "You're sure there's nothing on that body that could be linked back to us?"

"I'm positive," Ratchet says, finally looking at me. "I did my job."

"They've tried to take Ginny once. They may try again. We need to be doubly sure that Ginny is safe," Raze declares.

My stomach clenches at the mention of Ginny. "I'll take care of her," I say firmly. "She's with me now, and she's safe."

"Good," Raze says, nodding. "We'll focus on finding out who's after us and what we can do to protect ourselves."

The meeting goes on for another hour, with everyone throwing ideas out on how to proceed. By the time we're done, the tension in the room has eased somewhat, but I know things are far from resolved. We have bigger problems to deal with now, and we can't afford to make any mistakes.

As I leave the meeting, Ratchet falls into step beside me. "We need to talk," he says, his voice low.

I stop and turn to face him. "About what?"

"About Ginny. And about what happened in the kitchen."

I swallow hard, knowing this conversation is long overdue. "I'm sorry about what happened with Ginny," I say sincerely.

Ratchet narrows his eyes at me. "You think an apology is going to fix this?"

"No, I don't," I admit. "But it's a start."

"We have other shit we need to worry about right now, but I want to make myself clear. I know you care about my sister, and for some fucking reason, she seems to care about you. But this shit with Roman and now the Feds, it's more than just the issues between you and me. I need to know you're going to keep her safe."

"You know I will."

"You have to understand I have a responsibility to protect her too."

"I understand," I say, hoping he can see the genuine remorse in my eyes. "But you have to trust me, Ratchet. I would never do anything to hurt Ginny."

Ratchet studies me for a long moment before finally nodding. "Okay," he concedes. "But just know that I'll be watching you."

"I wouldn't expect any less," I say, relieved the tension between us has lifted somewhat.

"You owe me a deep clean of my kitchen, asshole. I fucking eat in there."

"Noted." I smile.

Ratchet heads off toward the common room where Ginny is sitting on the couch talking to Darcy, finally feeling better enough to visit. He stops to talk to her for a few minutes. The tension eases from her shoulders at the hope of his forgiveness.

Smith's phone vibrates in my left pocket, dragging me from the moment between them. I pull it out, a sigh escaping my lips. Sliding back into the meeting room, I take his call.

"Care to explain why one of my agents was just found dead in Death Valley?"

"Why would I know anything about that? Why would this man be connected with my club in any way unless you fucking ordered it?" My eyes stay trained in the common room. "Seems to me this is a *you* problem."

"I want answers, Mr. Sterling, and I want answers now. He had a fucking family."

"And so do I. But it didn't fucking stop you or your boss from going after her, did it?"

Smith silences on the other end. "You're walking a dangerous line, Lucas. One wrong step, and you'll take your little girlfriend down with you."

"Is that a threat?" I seethe.

"It's a promise."

The line goes dead.

Chapter 24

GINNY

PEERING INTO THE BATHROOM MIRROR, I run my hands over my belly, envisioning what I would look like with a swollen stomach. My fingers trace over my soft skin as I smile at the thought. I turn to admire my silhouette from the side, imagining the curve that will form as my body grows with new life.

The anxiety of the news fades away slowly, being replaced with excitement. I've never imagined myself as a mother, but now that the idea had taken hold, I can't shake it. I turn back to the mirror, gently pressing my hand against my stomach, wondering what it will feel like to have a life growing inside me.

The only problem is that I haven't told Lucas yet. We've never discussed having kids. I have no idea if this is something he even wants. I scarcely know my own thoughts on it until the decision has been made for me by nature taking its course.

I know I have to tell him, but the thought of his reaction makes me nervous. Will he be happy or feel trapped like he's being forced into something he doesn't want? I take a deep breath, trying to calm my nerves as I hear his footsteps approaching. I open the bathroom door and find him standing in front of me, a curious look on his face.

"Hey," he says, his voice low and husky. "What are you doing here? Is it your stomach again?"

"No, nothing like that. I'm fine. Well, I am still a little nauseous, but it's going away."

"Should I call Doc to see if he can give you something for it?"

"No, no." I wave him off. "It's fine."

"If it's fine, then why do you look so nervous, Gin? What's going on?"

"We need to talk," I say, suddenly feeling nervous all over again.

"Okay..." he says, still looking at me with a quizzical expression.

I take another deep breath and finally say those two words, "I'm pregnant."

"You can't be," he blurts out. "I thought you were on the shot. Did you lie to me?"

Hearing those words sting like a slap to the face.

It isn't what I expected. "No, I didn't lie," I reply, desperately trying to keep the tears from falling. "I don't know what happened. I'm not due for my next one for another couple of weeks."

Lucas stares at me in shock, his face contorted with anger and confusion. "How is this even possible, Gin?" His expression turns from confusion to anger. "Failed? How could it fail?"

"I don't know... it just did."

"We're careful. We're always careful."

Were we? We'd taken the chance that my birth control was effective, clearly underestimating how much Mother Nature can have her own plans for our bodies. "I know," I say, my voice trembling. "But accidents happen. I know it's not the best timing, but I thought you should know."

"And what are we supposed to do now?" Lucas snaps, pacing back and forth. "We're not ready for a kid, Gin. *Fuck!*" he roars. "This is the last thing we need right now."

"I know," I say softly, feeling more and more defeated with each passing moment. "But we'll figure it out. We always do."

He stops pacing and looks at me with a strange expression. "Do you even want this, Gin? Do you want to be a mother?"

The question catches me off guard, and for a

moment, I'm unsure how to answer. "I don't know," I say finally, feeling tears prick at the corners of my eyes. "But it's happening, whether we want it or not."

"It doesn't have to if you don't want this. I'm not ready for a kid right now."

I peer down at my stomach and the life growing inside me—the life we've created together. The thought of terminating our child because it's not convenient for us to have a baby right now is a sickening thought.

"I don't want to terminate it," I say, my voice barely above a whisper. "I know it's not the ideal situation, but I can't just get rid of it. It's a life, Lucas. Our child."

"What if this isn't what I want? Do I not get a say in this?"

His words smart. *How can he be so cruel?*

I take a deep breath and try to keep my emotions in check. "Of course, you have a say, Lucas. But this is my body, my choice. And I want to keep it. If you don't want to be involved, I understand. But please don't ask me to get rid of our child."

Lucas falls silent, his eyes flickering with a mix of emotions. "I just... I don't know how to be a father," he admits finally. "I don't know if I'm ready for this kind of responsibility."

"We'll figure it out… together," I say, taking his hand. "It won't be easy, but we can do this."

"I don't think I can, Gin. If this were another time, I'd be overjoyed, but there's so much at stake right now. You're already vulnerable. A baby makes it all the harder to protect you."

My heart shatters at his words.

I thought he'd be happy and excited to be a father, but now I realize I was foolish for thinking that way. The thought of having a baby has clouded my judgment, and I've forgotten that not everyone is ready for this kind of responsibility.

I take a deep breath, trying to compose myself. "I understand," I say softly, releasing his hand. "If you don't want to be involved, I won't force you to be."

"It's a little too late for that, isn't it?" he growls. "You've already decided for us."

I flinch at the harshness in his tone. This isn't how I wanted this conversation to go. I thought he'd at least be willing to discuss it with me, and we could figure out a plan together, but now, I see the gravity of the situation. This isn't just about me and my desire to be a mother. It's about us, as a couple, and whether or not we're ready for this kind of commitment. He may not be ready for this, but I think I am. I want this. I want this baby.

Tears streak down my face. "You don't have to be involved. I *can* and *will* do this on my own, Lucas."

"It's not that easy, Gin. You don't just decide to keep a baby like it's some kind of accessory. This is a life we're talking about, and what if we can't provide for it? What if we can't be good parents? Have you thought about that?"

"I have," I say, my voice firm. "And we'll figure it out. We have time to plan and prepare. I'm not saying it will be easy, but I can't just give this up. It's a part of me… of us."

Lucas runs his hands through his hair, his shoulders tense. "I need some time to process this, Gin. I need to figure out what I want and what's best for us."

"You mean what's best for *you*."

"No, I don't. I think about you. I always think about you. Have you considered what could happen if someone tries to take you again? What they could do to you and my child?"

"I haven't because it won't happen again," I fire back. "It was a one-time thing."

"You *don't know that*," he roars. "They could try again, and this time, I may not make it in time to save you."

"You're talking nonsense right now. Do you hear yourself?"

"If you knew what I was doing to keep you safe, you wouldn't even be considering this," he seethes.

I stare at him, my mind reeling. *What does he mean by that?* What could he be doing to keep me safe that would make me reconsider having a baby with him?

"What are you doing, Lucas?" I ask, my voice barely above a whisper. "What have you been hiding from me?"

His eyes flicker with something I can't quite place, but then he shakes his head. "It doesn't matter. Just know I'll do whatever it takes to keep you safe."

"That's not an answer," I say, my voice growing stronger. "You can't just throw out vague statements like that and expect me to be okay with it. I need to know what you're doing."

"Gin, please." He looks at me with pleading eyes, but I stand my ground.

"No. I need to know… especially now, with a baby on the way. I won't let anything happen to our child, but I can't do that if I don't know everything."

"I can't tell you," he says, his voice going softer. "Not yet, anyway. But I need you to trust me, Gin. Please."

I stare at him, unsure of what to do. I want to trust him, but his words were cryptic, leaving me with more questions than answers. What is he keeping from me? And why does it have anything to do with our baby? "I do trust you," I say finally, the words leaving a bitter taste in my mouth. "But you need to be honest with me. What are you doing?"

He hesitates for a moment before taking a deep breath. "I've been working on something," he says slowly. "Something that will protect you for the rest of your life. Something that will make sure no one can ever hurt you again."

I stare at him, trying to process his words. "What kind of *something*?" I ask, feeling the fear coil in my stomach.

"It's… complicated," he says, avoiding my gaze.

"Uncomplicate it."

"I can't, Gin."

Chapter 25

SLIDER

SHE'S PREGNANT.

Ginny is fucking pregnant with my baby, and Smith is breathing down my goddamn neck, slinging threats toward her. If she had any idea what I have been doing to keep her safe, she wouldn't even be considering this.

The idea of bringing a baby into this chaos scares me more than going back to prison. It's not the right time. Ginny has to see reason, but I know she won't. Before she even told me, she'd made her mind up.

I watch as Ginny's face lights up, her eyes shining with joy as she cradles her stomach. She is so happy, content, sure, and unaware of how close I've come to losing her.

She wants this baby.

I want her alive.

I can't think straight. My mind is clouded with thoughts of Smith, his threats, and our constant danger. How can I protect Ginny and our child from all of this? I have to come up with a plan and fast, and I need to think quickly. I can't let Smith find out about the baby. He'd stop at nothing to use it as leverage against me, forcing me to do more than plant cameras in V's office.

"I'm getting some air," I say.

The sadness on her face fucking kills me as I leave our room. I'm an asshole. A complete fucking asshole for even suggesting she terminate the pregnancy, but if she only knew what was at stake right now. How Smith could make a single phone call and take her life like snuffing out a burning flame. If she knew, she'd understand my hesitation, but I can't fucking tell her. I'd come so close, allowing the heat of the moment to strip away my restraint.

I take a deep breath, trying to clear my head, but the thoughts keep swirling in my mind like a whirlpool.

Think, asshole. Think.

I could leave town with Ginny and start over somewhere new, but would that really be safe? Smith has connections everywhere. He'd find us eventually. He managed to find Roman's remains within a week of his disappearance. Two adults and a baby would be child's play for him to track. Not to mention, Ratchet would scorch the entire Earth to find us on top of Smith. Running isn't going to work.

I need a better plan to keep Ginny and the baby safe while also taking care of Smith.

The answer stares me back in my face.

I can't leave, but Ginny can.

Leave me.

Leave the club.

Cut her ties from all of this.

I can do it.

I can make her believe I don't want her or the child. It will be the most painful thing I can ever do, but it's the only way to keep them both safe. Smith will lose his leverage, and I can devise a plan to take care of him without worrying about Ginny's life hanging in the balance.

I'll have to break her heart.

I hate myself for even considering it, but it's the only way.

Texting Ginny to meet me outside in ten minutes, I head into the common room, spotting who I need by the bar, chatting with one of the other girls. I hate myself for getting her mixed up in this, but she's the only one of the girls who will see this for what it is.

"Come with me."

She blinks at me. "What for?" Ruby asks, tilting her head slightly to the side.

I ignore her question and lean in closer, my voice low and intense. "Don't ask questions. Move."

Ruby nods, sensing the urgency in my voice, and starts to follow me toward the exit. I glance around the common room, making sure no one is following us before I whisper to Ruby, "I need you to do something for me."

"What?" Ruby asks, her eyes narrowing in suspicion.

"Get on your knees."

"What the hell, Slider?" Ruby hisses, her eyes blazing with anger. "Aren't you with Ginny?"

"I am," I reply through gritted teeth. "But I need you to do this for me." I grab her arm and pull her down to her knees. "Please. It's for Ginny's safety. I can't explain it now, but I need your help."

Ruby looks up at me, her expression softening as she reads the desperation on my face. She nods slowly, her hands reaching for my zipper. She shoves her hand inside, grasps my limp cock, and pulls it free. I want to recoil at her touch, but I've got to do this. I have to make Ginny believe what she's seeing in front of her is real.

"Are you sure about this?"

"Just fucking do it." I grasp the back of Ruby's

head, drawing her to me as the backdoor swings open. Ginny steps outside and witnesses the display in front of her—Ruby on her knees, my cock in her hand, and her mouth dangerously close to it.

"What the fuck are you doing?" Ginny seethes, her eyes wide and brimming with tears.

Ruby smiles from her position. "It's just a blow job, Ginny. You can have him back when I'm done."

"Get on with it," I say, my voice thick with emotion. It physically hurts to be saying these words, but I have to keep going. I have to drive it home. I drag Ruby's face closer, her hot breath warm against my still-flacid cock.

"Why are you doing this?" Ginny cries, tears streaking down her beautiful face. I can see the hurt and betrayal in her eyes. I want to break away from Ruby, explain it to her, and make her understand, but I can't. Not yet.

"Because I can," I hiss. "These girls are here for our use. I'm using her."

Ginny stares at me for a long moment before she turns and runs away toward her car. I hold Ruby in place until she speeds off out of sight. I stand stunned, my heart slipping away piece by piece with each passing second she's gone, but it's what had to be done.

Ruby stands, her hands shaking as I shove my

cock back inside my jeans. "Thank you," I say softly, my voice barely above a whisper. "I owe you one."

Ruby looks at me, her eyes filled with sadness and confusion. "What's going on, Slider?" she asks, her hand reaching out to touch my face.

"I can't explain it now," I say, stepping back from her touch. "If anyone asks, you blew me. Got it?" I leave Ruby there and head back inside, leaving my heart and fucking soul out there in the parking lot.

Ginny will hate me for the rest of my life.

My kid will be born and grow up without me

But I had to do it to keep them both safe.

Now, I only hope it is enough.

Chapter 26

GINNY

WHY WOULD he do this to us?

Why, after everything we've been through, would he throw it away for a fucking blow job?

I know he wasn't happy about the baby, but I thought he'd come around after the initial shock. I thought he loved me and was my future. We'd fought so hard to get back to each other. Clearly, I'd been wrong about everything.

I drive with no destination in mind, only the need to put distance between us. The tears are streaking down my face as my heart breaks into a million pieces. One road blurs into another until my brother's house comes into view. I quickly stop my car in front of the house, get out, and sprint up to the door.

Ricca, alerted by the noise, greets me as I enter. "Ginny, what's wrong?"

"Everything." I sob, my body giving up and falling into her.

Ricca wraps her arms around me, holding me close as I cry. She knows something isn't right but waits until I'm ready to talk, letting me sob on her shoulder. "Shh, it's okay. Whatever it is, we'll get through it together."

I finally pulled away, wiping my eyes with the back of my hand. "It's L-Lucas," I say, my voice cracking. "He cheated on me." The words burn. "He cheated on me," I choke out again.

Ricca's eyes widen before fierce anger takes hold. "He did what?"

"I caught him with Ruby." I sob, choking on my tears.

"That fucking asshole," she finally says, her voice low and filled with venom. "How could he do that to you?"

"I don't know." I keep crying. "I thought we were happy, and then I found out I'm pregnant. Now this."

"Wait. You're pregnant?"

I nod, wiping away the tears.

"Oh, Gin. I'm so sorry." My stomach churns, hearing my nickname from him, stabbing me in the heart further. Where it used to comfort me, it only serves as a reminder of what we've just lost. Ricca wraps her arms around me again, a low growl rumbling from her throat. "That bastard. He has no right to do this to you. I'm so sorry, Ginny. You deserve so much better."

I sob into her shoulder, finally feeling the weight of what happened settle over me. I cling to Ricca for comfort, cherishing her presence.

"What's going on?" my brother's voice cuts through my sobs behind us. "Ginny?"

I turn to face him, unable to hide the pain. He crosses the distance between us in three strides, taking my face between his hands. "What. Did. He. Do?" My brother's anger builds with each word.

"He cheated on me." The truth comes out in an anguished wail.

My brother's jaw sets, rage in every line of his body. "That son of a bitch," he spits out, his voice full of venom. "Tell me everything."

I recount what I'd seen. How Lucas looked at me like this wasn't something I should be concerned about. That the father of my child getting blown by another woman in front of me was nothing. That everything between us had been nothing.

My brother's face contorts in rage. He steps away, his hands balling into fists at his side. He looks like he's about to explode into a fit of rage. "I'm going to kill him."

Ricca grabs his arm, soothing him. "Let's not do

anything we'll regret," she says, her voice low and even.

"Killing him is not something I will regret. I warned him. I fucking warned him what would happen if he hurt her," he seethes, murderous rage flaring in his eyes.

"There's something else she needs to tell you, Jude."

My brother shifts his gaze back to me. "Is there fucking more? Did he hit you?" Jude shifts to me, his hands checking my face for any signs of bruising.

"No, he didn't hurt me. He would never lay a hand on me."

"Then what is it?"

"I'm pregnant."

Jude's body unnaturally stills. "Does he know that? For the love of fucking God, Ginny, please tell me he didn't know."

"He did." I sob as I nod. "I told him. We got into a fight and asked me about an abortion."

"He asked you to get rid of it?" The anger in my brother's face builds even more. "That's it. I'm going to kill him for real this time," he growls.

Ricca whirls on him. "No, Jude. Let's think of a better plan. You're not going to do something you'll regret. Besides, Ginny needs you now. She needs your protection and strength. You're the only one who can provide that for her."

My brother's face softens, and he pulls me in for a hug. "Shh… everything is going to be all right," he whispers into my hair. "We'll figure this out."

I knew my brother would do anything to protect my unborn child and me. I can't help but think if only Lucas had been as protective of me as my brother. The words of our fight about the baby come back to haunt me. He said he was trying to protect me. To save me from something I didn't know about yet and how a baby would make it more difficult. None of it makes sense.

"Where is he?" he asks me, searching my face. "Tell me where he is."

"The clubhouse."

"I'm going to fucking fix this, Ginny." My brother turns to Ricca, his voice low and urgent. "Stay with her. I'll be back soon."

He pivots on his heels and grabs his cut from the chair in the kitchen as he passes us. He pauses before the front door, looking back at me, rage clear on his face. Without another word, he slips through the door. The sound of his motorcycle roars to life soon after.

"No, wait!" Ricca calls out and leaves me. She runs for the door, but it's too late. My brother speeds past the front door in the direction of the clubhouse.

She watches until the sound fades away. "Fuck," she snarls.

"You don't think he means it, do you? About killing him?"

Ricca sighs, walking back to me. She wraps her arms around me, pulling me in close. "Your brother would burn the world for you, Ginny. Anything is possible."

Lucas broke my heart and destroyed everything between us.

But death? Can I be okay with that? Could I live with myself that *his* death would be on my hands? The death of the father of my child.

"I have to go after him. I can't let Jude do this." I push past her. I make it through the front door and down a few steps before she grabs my elbow, stopping me.

"No," Ricca demands. "Let him handle this. If you show up there, it'll only make matters worse. It will remind your brother just what he's done, and that's a surefire way of guaranteeing your worst fears."

I nod, tears streaming down my face. Ricca is right. This is between them now.

"Come on, let's go back inside. We'll figure out

what's going to happen from here. It's going to be all right," she soothes, her voice full of comfort.

"How will it be all right?" Nothing will be okay. My baby will grow up without a father either way.

"I don't know," she admits. "I really don't know."

I look at her, my heart beating hard. I know she's right, but I can't help but feel guilty for being powerless to help my brother or protect Lucas. My shoulders slump. She's right. I've done enough damage, but I'm already reaching for my phone. I need to ensure nothing happens to Lucas. I need to protect my baby's father, no matter how much I might hate him right now.

He knows.

Ricca feels the hesitation in my shoulders. "I know it seems bleak right now, but I promise you, it will be okay."

I nod, leaning into her shoulder.

"Do you know what will make you feel better?"

I peer at her from her shoulder, a small smile on her face.

"What?"

"Mint chocolate chip ice cream. I picked up a couple of pints on my way home from the security office yesterday. They have your name on it."

"Is there marshmallow fluff?"

Ricca shakes her head, laughing. "I don't know what's weirder… your love for chocolate toothpaste-flavored ice cream or the fact that you and your brother are clones when it comes to adding marsh-mallow fluff onto ice cream? Fucking weirdos."

Together, we turn and head back inside.

I'm grateful she's here to pick up the pieces of my broken heart.

Chapter 27

SLIDER

EVEN BEFORE GINNY'S unexpected warning, I knew he'd be here. I knew he would come to defend his sister's honor. I'd expected and planned for it to make this believable. It's inevitable.

I hear the motorcycle before I see him. Ratchet skids into the parking lot, his bike not even at a full stop before he's off it and charging in my direction.

"You *son of a bitch*," he roars. He doesn't stop. He swings wide, a haymaker coming at the force of a speeding bullet train for my face. I don't move. I don't dodge. I allow it to connect.

Pain explodes across my jaw, and I feel my head snap back. I fall to the ground, and he's on me, his boot colliding with my ribs. I gasp for air, trying to pull away from him, but he grabs a fistful of my hair and slams my head onto the concrete. The world goes dark for a moment.

When I come to, he's straddling me, his hands around my throat. His face is contorted in rage, his eyes burning holes in my skull. I try to push him off, but his grip only tightens.

I deserve his punishment.

I deserve it for what I had to do to keep Ginny safe.

"You think you can just walk away from her?" he hisses, spittle flying from his lips. "You think you can just leave her high and dry, pregnant with your fucking kid?"

I can't breathe, my vision starts to swim, and I feel myself slipping away again—a welcoming darkness to end this pain and anguish I feel for what I did. And then, suddenly, he lets go. I suck in a huge gulp of air, my chest heaving. He stands up, his knuckles bloody.

Raze stands behind him. His arms around his neck as he struggles to break away from him to get back to killing me.

"What the fuck is going on?"

I stumble back to my feet with my hand on my cheek, the world spinning around me. The pain radiates, blood pools in my mouth, and I spit it out on the ground, testing to make sure all of my teeth are still intact. Luckily they are.

"I'm going to fucking kill him."

"I can see that. Care to explain?" Raze demands, turning to me.

Ratchet answers for me. "He fucking cheated on Ginny." Ratchet is breathing hard, his eyes wild with anger. "You fucking hurt my sister, asshole," he says, spit flying from his mouth.

"I know," I admit.

Raze sighs. "Let's all calm down for a second. We can sort this out without anyone getting their asses kicked."

"She's pregnant."

Raze's eyes snap to mine. "Is this true?"

"She fucking told him, and he told her to get rid of it."

Guilt at my words being thrown back at me hurts worse than my face. I want that baby. I want it with Ginny so bad I can fucking taste it. But until Smith is dealt with, I don't have a choice. She has to stay away from me and the club.

Ratchet breaks free and charges again. His arms wrap around my stomach, spearing me back onto the parking lot's hard gravel. It rips into my flesh, little bits of stone embedding into the back of my forearms.

"You fucking bastard," he growls, his face hovering over mine. "You should have never done this to her, and you sure as fuck shouldn't have asked her to get rid of it."

"I know," I answer.

"You know?" he snarls in return. His hands clamp around my throat again, and his fingers dig into my flesh as he cuts off my air. I don't fight back, welcoming whatever fate is before me. If I weren't here, it would solve a lot of fucking problems.

Raze's hand claps down onto Ratchet's neck, pulling him away from me. "Enough," he growls.

Ratchet snarls but gets to his feet, standing above me.

"I'm going to release you, and you're going to walk away. Do you understand me?" Ratchet sneers at me. "Do you fucking understand me, Ratchet?"

"Yes," he bellows. Raze releases him, but Ratchet doesn't move, his eyes boring down on me on the ground. There's a calculating look on his face as if he's trying to figure out how to kill me before Raze stops him.

"You," he snarls at Ratchet. "Get the fuck out."

"This isn't over," he warns. "Stay the fuck away from my sister and the baby. You so as much look in her direction, I will fucking kill you."

"Out," Raze snarls.

Ratchet spits on me before he pivots on his heels. The roar of his bike is deafening before he speeds off, leaving Raze and me alone. I stay on the ground, not sure what to do.

Raze looks down at me. "You okay?"

"I've been better," I remark, getting to my feet. The world is still spinning.

Raze shakes his head as if he's disappointed. "Do I need to call Doc?"

My hand presses to the back of my head. Withdrawing it, I find my hand clean. Even though it feels like he split my head open, it isn't bleeding. "I'm fine." I try to walk away but stagger three steps in.

Raze grabs me, steadying me. "I think you and I need to talk."

He leads me inside. The rest of the guys littering the common room become silent as we enter.

"The fuck happened to him?" Hero calls out.

Raze doesn't answer, instead leading me down the hallway to his office. He helps me to one of the large chairs across from his desk, then settles into his chair, his hands drawn in front of him.

I feel like my world is spiraling out of control. Ratchet is out for my blood, Smith is breathing down my neck, and I'm unsure what to do next. I'm in uncharted waters, and I'm not sure how to navigate them. All I know is I need to keep Ginny and our unborn baby safe. I hope it's enough.

"Care to explain to me what's going on?"

I take a deep breath before I begin, "Nothing."

Raze leans forward. "I just stopped Ratchet from killing you in our fucking parking lot. It didn't look like nothing."

I want to tell him.

I want to tell him everything about Smith and why I hurt Ginny.

The need to do so is burning like an inferno in my throat, but I can't. Doing so will put us all in danger, not just me.

"It doesn't matter," I finally say. "It's just a misunderstanding," I finally answer.

Raze stares at me for a moment, then leans back in his chair. "A misunderstanding that almost resulted in your murder. I don't know why you did what you did, but I will not tolerate bringing this bullshit to the clubhouse." He pauses, his expression understanding.

I give a weak smile. "I'm sorry," I murmur.

"I know," he replies. "But I'm not here to forgive you. You two need to work your shit out. I won't have you two at each other's throats. We don't need that on top of everything else going on right now."

I nod. I know he's right. Ratchet is a loose cannon,

and he won't forget what I did, but right now, there is no way to fix it, but I offer, "I'll talk to him."

Raze shakes his head. "No. I'll talk to him. You're going to stay away from him. You need to keep your head down. I'll take care of this."

I nod.

"One more thing… Ginny."

"What about her?"

"I'm not one for getting myself involved in the relationships of our club members, but I guess I'm breaking my own fucking rules today. Whatever happened, happened. But you need to consider the baby. You need to man up and take responsibility."

I take a deep breath. "I understand," I reply, and Raze nods.

"Good. Don't waste it. I know mistakes happen. I've sure as fuck made them when it comes to a woman, but you need to consider that it's not just her in the equation."

He stands, indicating our conversation is over.

I thank him before heading back to my room, filled with guilt and shame. I know I need to do the right thing, but I'm not sure what that is. The only thing I'm sure of is I need to finish what I've started.

This shit with Smith needs to end.

Now.

Chapter 28

I'VE BARELY LEFT my room since Jude returned from the clubhouse with blood staining his knuckles and hands—Lucas' blood. I didn't ask what happened, only if he was still alive. My brother's answer of "for now" is reassurance enough that he is still breathing. The thought of his death being on my hands is nearly too much to bear, let alone the hatred I feel for myself that I still care he's alive.

He broke my heart, yet I still love him no matter how hard I try not to.

Ricca had tried for days to tempt me to leave my room. At first, it was my favorite meals, of which I could only stomach a few bites off the plate she brought me, and then, she sent Asher. It broke my heart to refuse him. I couldn't even face myself, let alone someone else. Every time I closed my eyes, I saw Lucas' face, battered and bruised, staring up at me in fear.

I knew I had to face Jude eventually, knowing he would be the only one who could give me the answers I sought, but first, I needed to find the courage to leave the safety of my room.

There is a knock at my door. I don't even bother to get up and answer it. I assume it's Ricca or Asher checking in on me once again.

"Go away."

"Someone's here to see you," Ricca says.

I bury my face into my pillow. "I don't want to see him."

"It's not Lucas," a deep voice responds for her. Peering from my pillow, I see Raze standing in the doorframe, his large build and height taking up much of the open space. "Can we talk?"

"Sure," I mutter, wiping away the tears from my face. I try to straighten my messy hair, but it's no use. Raze enters, nodding in thanks to Ricca.

I slide my feet from the bed. "What are you doing here?"

"I came to see how you are doing."

"I'm fine," I mutter. My default answer has been on repeat the last few days. I'm far from fine, but what else do I say? That the man I love broke my heart. Abandoned our child and me for a club whore.

There's nothing I can say to take away the pain he inflicted on us.

Raze's eyes search mine. "You don't have to be fine, you know. It's okay not to be okay."

"I know," I say, trying to steady my voice. "It's just hard."

"I can only imagine," he replies, coming to sit next to me on the bed. "But I want you to know you don't have to go through this alone. We're all here for you."

I feel a lump form in my throat, and the tears threaten to spill over again. Raze's kind words are overwhelming and remind me of what I've lost.

I turn back to face him, my eyes meeting his. "What do you mean?"

"I mean the club and the ladies."

"I don't understand. I'm not a part of the club anymore. Honestly, I don't know if I ever was."

"You'll always be a part of our family, Ginny." Raze takes a deep breath, his expression turning serious. "Has your brother ever mentioned my ex-wife?"

"You were married before Darcy?" I admit. "I just assumed you two had been together for a while."

Raze smiles. "That's story for another time. I have two kids with my ex. Harley, who's in college now, and Ky, who you may have seen at the party."

"Was he the one playing V's Switch?"

"That would be the one." He chuckles. "Kid loves to fuck with V. Chip off the ol' block, let me tell you. Anyway, I was married to their mom for a long fucking time. It was great at first. Harley came, and then a few years later, Ky was born. Our relationship went up in fucking smoke after he was born."

I shift on the bed.

Raze sighs before he continues with his story, "After Ky was born, she changed. It was gradual at first, going out with some of the ladies from the club… members now passed on. Next, she wouldn't come home for days on end. Thing is… I knew she was fucking cheating on me, and I'll be honest, I wasn't exactly faithful in my marriage after that either."

"Did you leave her?"

"I didn't." He sighs, the leather of his cut creaking as he shifts. "I stayed for my kids, knowing my ex was far from the mothering type. The thing is, they're not biologically mine."

I straighten in my seat. "Do they know?"

Raze shakes his head. "They don't, and outside of Dani, Darcy, and now, you, you're the only people who do know."

"Why would you tell me this?"

"Because no matter what happens between you and Slider, your baby is a part of you. You are its mother, and that bond is unbreakable. I should have left. Maybe if I had, Harley and Ky wouldn't have gone through the shit they had because of their mom, but I can't go back and change what happened. No one has the power to do that."

I swallow hard, the weight of his words sinking in. "Thank you, Raze."

"Of course," he says with a small smile. "But I want you to know something else too. You are strong enough to get through this. You may not feel it now, but you will. I spent sixteen years thinking my kids were mine, without a doubt. Now that I know they aren't, I don't love them any less. Same goes for Darcy and her kids."

"But, Roxie calls you Daddy?"

"She does." He nods. "Her dad, my best friend, died before she was born. I'm the only father figure she's ever known, and if Brent can't be here for her, I'm glad to be the one she calls Dad. The same will go for your baby. Whether Slider gets his head out of his ass or not, whoever they call their dad will love them just as much. Because if they don't, you have an entire club of men behind you to kick their ass to the curb."

"Thank you, Raze," I say again.

"You have your entire life ahead of you… a clean slate to be who you want to be." He gives my hand a reassuring squeeze before standing up, ready to leave. "Take care of yourself, Ginny. And remember, we've got your back."

I watch as he exits the room, feeling a faint glimmer of hope within me.

He's right.

My entire life is ahead of me.

And if I have nothing tying me here, maybe it's time I spread my wings and fly.

Chapter 29

SLIDER

WITH GINNY away from the clubhouse, I shift my focus to the flash drive. I spend hours and hours watching V work in his office with, thankfully, no repeat visits from his wife.

It wasn't until yesterday that I finally hit pay dirt. V opened the flash drive, and images I had no idea existed from Mexico popped up on the monitors in front of him. As a new prospect, Raze had opted to leave me behind. I knew shit had gone south there, but this is something far beyond what I expected— image after image of destruction and death, including a man in lime green shoes and a woman with a bullet wound to her forehead.

What the hell had happened down there?

I watched as Raze joined him. I sat for over an

hour, recording the photographs and their damning conversation. He'd given me enough that maybe, just fucking maybe, it would be what Smith needed, enough that I could get out from underneath his goddamn thumb.

After transferring the images to a new flash drive, I use my burner phone to call the asshole. "I have what you want."

"Good, Mr. Sterling. I happen to be in town." I hear muffled voices in the background and the rustle of papers being shifted around. "Meet me at the, uh… there's a pull-off just south of Mt. Baldy Village. Do you know it?"

"Yeah," I admit.

"One hour," he demands. "See you soon, Mr. Sterling."

I hang up the phone and take a deep breath, trying to calm my racing heart. I know meeting with Smith is dangerous, but I've gone too far down this road to turn back now. I have to do this for Ginny and our baby. I willingly broke her heart for this. There is no turning back now.

I grab my keys and make my way out of the clubhouse. The sun has just set, casting an eerie glow over the twists and turns of the mountain roads.

As I ride toward the pull-off, I can't shake the feeling I'm being followed. My eyes dart behind me at every turn and stoplight, searching for any sign of danger.

Finally, I arrive at the pull-off. I park my bike and nervously wait for Smith to arrive. It only takes a few minutes before I hear the sound of a car approaching. I peer through the darkness, trying to make out the vehicle. It's a black SUV with tinted windows and no license plates.

My heart races as I watch the driver's side door open, and Smith steps out.

"You look like you've been through a fucking cheese grater," Smith remarks with a cocky smile. "Who'd you piss off?"

"None of your fucking business, Smith," I hiss.

"Where's your girlfriend? I'm surprised you didn't have her tag along to keep an eye on her with me in town."

I glare at him.

"Oh, trouble in paradise, eh?"

"That's none of your concern," I reply curtly.

"Ah, all right then. Just trying to be friendly," Smith says, raising his hands in mock surrender. "Point taken. Do you have what I want?"

Pulling the new flash from my back pocket, I shove it into his hand.

"What's this?" he says, rolling the flash drive in his fingers.

"What you wanted. Proof of the club's involvement in the Manuel Cartel."

Smith's eyes widen in surprise as he examines the flash drive. "Well, well, well," he mutters under his breath. "Seems like you've delivered on your promise. Though, I'd be an idiot to accept this as is. What's to say this flash drive isn't empty?"

"Check it," I shrug. "It's there."

"Well, see about that."

He motions behind him. Two men in identical black suits step from the back seat of the SUV, one carrying a laptop. They reach Smith, who hands the flash drive over his shoulder. His buddy plugs it into the computer. After a few clicks, Raze's voice comes from the laptop's speakers.

Smith's mouth curves upward into a smile. "Well, I'll be damned."

I feel a knot form in my stomach. I've just handed over my club on a silver platter, knowing that Smith can now move on the club and my actions will rip apart their families and lives.

What the fuck have I done?

I clench my fists, feeling the bile rise in my throat.

"You certainly didn't disappoint me, Sterling," Smith says, still grinning. "I'll be in touch."

"The fuck you will. This is done. I did what you asked," I fire back.

"This is *far* from over." Smith's smirk widens as he takes a step closer to me.

"I held up my end of the bargain. You have what you want, Smith."

"This is a start."

A start?

A fucking start!

He has the proof he needs—photographs and a fucking conversation with Raze, implicating himself in the murders of that cartel. It's all right there on that flash drive.

Smith steps even closer, his breath hot on my face. "You seem nervous, Sterling. Need some reassurance?"

I back away from him, feeling the cool metal of my bike against my legs. "I don't need anything from you."

Smith's eyes darken, and he takes another step closer, his hand reaching out to grab my shirt. "You know, Mr. Sterling, I have a feeling you're not telling me everything."

I stiffen, my hand subconsciously inching toward the knife in my boot. At this angle, it would be hard to stab him, but not impossible if the need arises. "What are you talking about?"

He leans in, his breath hot against my ear. I feel the anger and frustration boiling inside me. I put everything on the line for Ginny and our future, and here I am being accused of keeping secrets. I betrayed my club for this shit.

"You're hiding something from me, Mr. Sterling," he whispers, his grip on my shirt tightening.

"I don't know what the hell you're talking about," I spit out, trying to pull away from him, but his grip on my shirt only tightens.

"Don't lie to me," he growls, his eyes blazing with anger. "I know you've been withholding information. And if you don't tell me what it is right now, I swear to God I'll make you regret it."

"I've given you everything I have," I retort, my heart pounding hard. "What more do you want?"

"Everything," he snarls, shoving me back against my bike. "I want to know everything there is to know about your goddamn club. And if you don't give it to me willingly, I'll take it by force."

I glare at Smith, unimpressed. "I want out. I did what you asked, and now I want out of this. I want the deal we made."

Smith laughs, the sound grating on my nerves.

"You really are new to this game, aren't you? There are no deals in this world… only power. And right now, I have *all the power*. I damn well own you."

He holds my gaze a second longer before turning away, his entourage quickly following suit.

"I'll be in touch, Mr. Sterling," he says, throwing a final glance over his shoulder.

And then he's gone, leaving me alone, surrounded by darkness and uncertainty.

What have I done?

Chapter 30

GINNY

"THANK YOU FOR COMING WITH ME." I smile at Darcy in the passenger seat. "I'm a little nervous."

While I wanted to ask Ricca, I couldn't bring myself to put her through this. She'd once told me kids would never be in the cards for her and my brother, and caring for her little brother would be the closest thing they'd ever have to a child. I'd talked to Jude about inviting her, but he agreed it would be best if I asked someone else. Thankfully, Darcy was available and happy to tag along with me.

"It's understandable. I still remember my first prenatal appointment. I was scared out of my mind, and when they pulled out the ultrasound wand, I thought about bolting right then and there."

As we pull up in front of the building, I can feel

my heart racing. Darcy reaches over and gives my hand a reassuring squeeze.

"Don't worry, you'll do great. And if all else fails, we'll go get virgin margaritas afterward." She grins.

I laugh, grateful for her humor. I take a deep breath, open the car door, and step out into the warm summer air. Darcy is right beside me as we make our way inside to the waiting room across from the building's entrance.

The OBGYN office is a cheery bright yellow. Pictures of babies fill a few cork boards by the reception area—the happy, chubby faces of the newborns they'd helped to bring into this world.

I look around at the other women with various degrees of rounded bellies. Each of them is here with a man. I check myself in, take the paperwork the receptionist gives me, and fill it out.

My thoughts are interrupted as the receptionist calls my name, signaling it's my turn to be seen. Darcy gives my hand another reassuring squeeze before settling into one of the chairs.

The nurse opens the door to the exam rooms and ushers me in.

"I'm Ashlee, one of Dr. Richards' nurses."

She shows me to a scale, prompting me to step on it before leading me to the restroom a few doors down then hands me a plastic cup.

"I already had a positive pregnancy test," I tell her.

"Standard procedure." She shrugs, putting the cup in my hand. "There's a little door along the left wall. Once you're done, just set it inside, and I'll take care of it from there."

I open the restroom door. The motion sensor light kicks on, illuminating the room. Doing as she asked, I pee into the cup and place it in the spot she mentioned. After washing my hands, I step outside to find Ashlee waiting for me. She leads me into an open exam room.

"Please change into this and hop up on the table." Ashlee points to the cotton gown lying on the exam table. She disappears out the door immediately after.

I change into the cotton gown, feeling exposed and vulnerable. My heart races with anticipation as I hear a knock before the door opens and the doctor enters.

"Hello, I'm Dr. Richards," he introduces himself with a warm smile.

"Hi, I'm Ginny," I reply, trying to sound calm despite my nerves.

"So, this is your first pregnancy," he says, reviewing the paperwork I handed to the receptionist when I was called back.

"Yes, it is," I confirm. He then goes over my

medical history—the date of my last period, my medications, and the sparse family history I can give him.

"And you were actively taking a preventive when you discovered your pregnancy?"

"Yes. The shot."

Surprise fills his face. "While uncommon, it does happen. Though, I have to caution you it is possible this is a chemical pregnancy."

I feel a jolt of panic run down my spine at his words, but I try to keep my voice steady. "What does that mean?"

"It means that the pregnancy may not be viable, and your body may naturally terminate the pregnancy on its own without any intervention," he explains. "But let's not jump to conclusions just yet. First, I need to check and see where you're at in your pregnancy. The ultrasound will give us a more accurate picture."

He motions for me to lie back on the exam table. As he starts the exam, his touch is surprisingly gentle, which puts me at ease.

"So far, everything looks good, but we'll do an ultrasound just to make sure," he says as he finishes the exam.

As he sets up the machine, I feel my nerves returning. I grip the edge of the table tightly, trying to steady myself. He turns, and the wand Darcy had mentioned earlier is in his hand. He slides on a condom before slathering lubrication onto the wand. The thought of bolting definitely comes to mind.

"Here we go," he says, turning on the machine. The room fills with the sound of the ultrasound waves, and my heart races with anticipation.

Suddenly, I see it—the tiny little flutter that is my baby's heartbeat. Tears fill my eyes as I stare at the screen, finally realizing I am going to be a mother.

"It looks like the fetus is healthy and right on track," the doctor says, breaking my thoughts as he turns off the machine. "You're measuring around six weeks, which puts your due date around the end of February or early March."

He turns to the machine, hitting a few keys. A strip of black and white images appears. He rips the paper off, handing it to me.

"This is my baby?" I ask, my eyes unable to look away from the small bundle in the middle of the each image.

"It is," he smiles. "Congratulations."

As I clutch the ultrasound pictures in my hand, my mind races with thoughts of what life will be like once the baby arrives. So many unknowns fill my head, but the one thing that remains certain is my love for this tiny life growing inside me.

"Thank you so much, Dr. Richards," I say, my voice shaking with emotion. "I can't tell you how much this means to me."

"It's my pleasure," he replies with a warm smile. "And just remember, we're here to support you every step of the way. I'll let you change, and Ashlee will be in to schedule your next appointments and follow-up bloodwork. I'd like to get you started on prenatal vitamins. I'll send you home with some samples to try."

As he exits the room, I gather my thoughts and quietly wipe away the tears streaming down my face. *I am going to be a mother.* The thought fills me with excitement and trepidation all at the same time. *What will my life be like with a baby? Will I be a good mother?* These questions race through my mind as I change back into my clothes.

When I step back into the exam room, Ashlee is waiting for me with a small paper bag in her hands. "Here you go, Ginny. These are the prenatal vitamins that Dr. Richards recommends. Start taking one every day, and we'll go over the rest of your appointments when you're ready."

I take the bag from her, nodding my acknowledgment. "Thank you, Ashlee."

As I leave the exam room and head back to the waiting area, I can't help but feel a sense of relief wash over me. The ultrasound has confirmed my pregnancy, and knowing that my baby is healthy, I feel a newfound confidence as a mother-to-be.

Darcy stands as I approach her, taking the ultrasound pictures from my hand. "Oh my God, Ginny! Look at how tiny your baby is," she exclaims, her eyes filling with tears.

We embrace in a tight hug, our tears of joy mingling together.

As we pull away from each other, I can't help but feel grateful to have Darcy by my side. She has been my rock throughout this whole process.

"So, what now?" she asks me as we leave the doctor's office.

"Now, we plan and prepare for the baby," I reply, feeling a renewed sense of purpose.

Darcy nods in agreement. "I can't wait to be an auntie," she says with a smile. "I am going to be the auntie, right?"

I nod my head, smiling. "This little one is going to have a lot of aunties and uncles."

"That they will. Big scary uncles."

In my car, Darcy chatters away, throwing out baby names as we drive toward her house. We make plans for a girls' lunch to celebrate before she heads inside her house. I pull away, heading back toward my brother's.

My heart drops when I spy the clubhouse on the left. I peer over to the ultrasound images sticking out of my purse and back again as I pass it. A few of the guys are in the parking lot as I pass and my heart hammers in my chest. Thankfully, Lucas isn't one of them.

I make it back to my brother's house, parking the car outside. I pull the images from my purse, my finger stroking the life growing inside me.

I'm going to be a mother.

I'm responsible for this tiny life growing inside of me.

A wave of anxiety washes over me, and I feel tears prick at the corners of my eyes.

"I have to keep you safe," I whisper to my stomach. I peer over to my brother's house, knowing what I have to do.

I have to take my baby as far away as I can from this club and Lucas. It's the only chance we have to live a safe and happy life.

We have to leave.

But even as I make peace with the decision, I know there's one thing I have to do before I go.

Chapter 31

SLIDER

GUILT CONTINUES to eat away at me. Every noise around the clubhouse puts me on high alert. It's been nearly a week since I met Smith at Mt. Baldy Village, and he's been radio silent. Something I would have welcomed before the flash drive, but now, dread builds with each passing second. The longer he stays quiet, the more anxious I become. He has what he needs to take down the club on that flash drive. He has it in spades, but yet he hasn't made his move.

Even with the club on high alert and Raze's daily meetings for updates on Roman Ward, my mind can't focus. Between Smith, Ginny, and the baby, I've found my limit of heartache and guilt.

I know I made a mistake by giving Smith that flash drive.

A mistake I am going to have to live with for the rest of my life, however long or short it is.

"Looks like you have a visitor," Tyson mutters, dragging me away from the whiskey I've been drowning myself in at the bar. I turn on my barstool. My heart thumps in my throat, expecting to see Smith behind me.

Only it's not Smith.

It's Ginny.

The sight of her makes my growing ache to hold her even worse than it was this morning when I fisted my cock in the shower at the thought of her pretty lips wrapped around it. I miss her. I miss waking up to her in my bed, her voice, her smile, and the way she says my name when she comes around my cock.

My mind goes blank, and I'm lost for words when I see Ginny standing there. She's dressed in a light-blue sundress that accentuates every curve of her toned body. Her raven hair is falling over her shoulders.

"Hi," I stutter out.

"You have a second to talk?" she answers, her voice wavering with each word.

"Yeah, sure," I stumble over myself.

She leaves the common room, heading out the

backdoor toward the parking lot, away from prying eyes.

"I'm sorry for coming here uninvited," she starts.

"This is your home just as much as it is mine, Ginny. You don't need an invitation to be here," I reply. "Your brother isn't with you, is he?" I peer around the parking lot, praying he isn't hiding in the bushes or behind a car to ambush me. His threat had been clear.

"No," she answers, taking a deep breath. "I brought you this." She pulls out a photograph from her purse and hands it to me. The image is black and white with a black V-shape and a white blob in the center of it.

"That's our baby." Her slender finger points to the blob.

"Our baby," I mutter, unable to tear myself away from the image. Our baby—the life growing inside Ginny's womb—our miracle. The excitement is soon overtaken by guilt. This is what I've given up. This is the price to keep her safe—a life without my baby and Ginny.

"I thought you'd want a copy."

"Thank you," I mutter, tucking it into my pocket.

"I thought you should have it since I'm leaving soon."

"Leaving?"

"Yes, I'm leaving California."

Hearing her say the words out loud is like a punch to the gut. This is what I wanted and my plan all along. So why did it hurt so much to hear her say the words?

"Where are you going?" My voice is barely above a whisper.

"Does it matter?"

It does, but I'm unable to say the words and tell her the truth that the thought of her leaving is killing me inside like a slow-acting poison I have administered to myself.

"When?"

"You don't deserve that answer." Ginny turns, taking a few steps, but turns back around. "Can I ask you why? Why did you throw away what we had? Can you at least give me that?"

"I can't," I force out and turn away from her. I don't want her to know the truth. I want her to go, to be safe from Smith and his threats. I want her to find the happiness she deserves and give our baby a good life. But now she's standing before me, I want her to stay and tell her everything.

"Why am I not surprised?" Ginny sighs. "Good-bye, Lucas."

I hear her turn to leave, but I reach out, grabbing

her elbow. Ginny jerks away from my grasp like my touch burns her.

"What are you doing?" I draw her near, throwing caution to the wind one last time. "What the hell are you doing? Let me go."

"I will, Gin. I am going to let you go." My throat tightens as the words hang between us. She struggles against my grasp. "You don't deserve to be dragged down with me. You deserve something better than this life."

"You don't get to decide what I deserve. That's *my* choice. I choose to give our baby a better life without you to taint it. Our baby deserves a better father than you," she snarls.

The pain in her voice is too much.

I can't do this anymore.

My hand releases her elbow. "I'm sorry, Gin," I utter. "For all of it."

Something inside me breaks, and I kiss her with everything I have. I pour all of my love into that kiss, trying to take away her pain and forge our final kiss into a memory to carry me forward.

Ginny pulls away, the sting of a slap coming across my face. "No!" she yells, her fingers pointing at me. I watch as she steps back, my heart breaking with each step. "I hate you," she seethes.

I hate myself more for what I have to do and have

had to give up. Her hatred is nothing compared to my own.

"I love you," I whisper. "I'll always fucking love you, Gin."

The image of our baby is burning a hole in my pocket as I watch Ginny's retreat until she disappears around the corner. My heart is heavy with guilt, but I know I have made the right decision for Ginny, even though it feels so wrong. Every fiber of my being is screaming for me to go after her.

I will never forget what we had, what we almost could have been.

Maybe someday, I'll find peace in knowing she's living her life to its fullest.

But today is not that day.

I can't force myself to look away as she speeds out of the parking lot, unable to reconcile she'll be gone. I don't know how long I stand here. Seconds. Minutes. Hours. All of it blurring together. The sting of her slap is still fresh on my cheek, and I savor the taste of her lips on mine one last time.

"Was that Ginny?" V asks, snapping me out of my trance as he rounds the corner with a cardboard box in his hand.

"Yeah," I answer flatly.

"She come to kick your ass too?" he jokes.

"No. She came to say goodbye."

I glance toward the empty parking lot once more.

"Goodbye." The word rings in my ears like a church bell.

"You could always go after her. I hear grand gestures are the way back into a woman's heart. It worked for me." He shrugs. "Worth the shot even if Ratchet will kill you for it."

"She's better off," I admit.

"If you say so." V continues on his way with his box, disappearing around the side of the building.

I slump against the building. My back slides down the exterior until my ass connects with the gravel. My head falls into my hands, a sob breaking through my walls before I can stop it.

I sit there, drowning in my grief, until Smith's phone vibrates in my pocket. I drag it out. A text message with two words pops up on the screen.

Tomorrow. Be ready.

Chapter 32

SLIDER

THE SMELL of gas permeates my nose. The strong sulfur odor takes over the space as I douse the couches with gasoline. Guilt rides me hard for what I am about to do. The consequences of my deal with Smith fully coming home to roost.

With the clubhouse cleared out after Smith tipped me off about the club's impending raid, I had my chance to do what needed to be done without harming anyone else in the process. The only solace I have with this final task.

I pull out the box of matches from my pocket, staring at them. My fingers tremble as I take one, the red end staring at me in condemnation. I sigh, moving it to the edge of the box to strike it when the side door flies open. Ratchet steps inside. His hand covers his mouth instantly before he catches me red-handed.

"What the fuck are you doing?"

"I'm doing what needs to be done," I reply, my voice steady as I light the match and toss it.

Ratchet charges for me, his attempt too late when the match hits one of the couches. The gas ignites with a whoosh, erupting in red and blue flames. The couches go up fast, smoke pouring into the room. The flames spread, speeding down the hallway toward the pile of towels I soaked with another can of gas that lies in the center of the office hallway.

We both hit the ground with a thud as the heat from the flames engulfs us. I struggle against his grip, but he's too strong for me. The heat is becoming intense, the flames now licking at the walls.

"Are you fucking trying to kill us all?"

"I made sure everyone was out," I say, desperate to convince him. "I checked every room before I started."

"Why?" he orders. "Tell me fucking why."

"I had no other choice," I say, my voice quivering as I try to catch my breath.

Ratchet's eyes widen in shock, but before he can say anything, the sound of sirens pierces through the chaos. His eyes snap to me. I can hear the sounds of shouts and orders being demanded from outside.

"You're the fucking rat."

Fear grips me as I know I've been caught. My heart races in my chest as I watch Ratchet's face twist in rage.

"I had *no choice!*" I shout back at Ratchet. "They found out about us, about the club. They were going to take us all down. I did what I had to do to protect us... to protect Ginny. They were going to kill her."

Ratchet's grip loosens, and for a moment, I think I have gotten through to him. But then, something in his eyes changes, and I realize my fate is sealed.

He stands, pulling me to my feet with him. "You're nothing but a fucking coward," he spits at me. "You sold us out for your own fucking self-preservation."

I try to protest, but he cuts me off with a hard punch to the face. I stumble back, falling against the wall as he advances on me with the intense fire burning around us.

Ratchet grabs me by the collar, pulling me close. "You're not getting out of this alive," he snarls. "You just signed your death warrant. It's fucking over for you." He rears back, his fist connecting with my face repeatedly until darkness dots my vision. He finally releases me, dragging my almost lifeless body to the center of the room, dropping me there on my back. He stands over me with a sneer on his face. "Enjoy hell, you fucking rat." He shifts from above me, disappearing into the smoke.

I watch as the fire licks hungrily at the walls and ceiling, the sound of crackling flames filling the air. Despite the intense heat, I don't move, my gaze transfixed on the inferno that was once our safe haven. Now I understand why Ratchet's calling card is fire—it's beautiful destruction springs forth new life in its aftermath.

The world around me darkens, my vision blurring from smoke and blood. Somewhere in the distant flames, I hear the door being kicked open and shouts and demands coming from inside the building, but I can't bring myself to care.

Chapter 33

GINNY

PACKING up a box of my belongings, I stare at the small pile forming next to my bedroom door.

Ricca appears in the doorway, twisting her dark hair as she plays with the ends of it. "Are you sure this is what you want?" she asks.

"I am. It's for the best." I wish I believed the words coming out of my mouth. The kiss from Lucas still sears my lips. My body craves his touch like a man dying of thirst. None of that can change what happened.

He cheated.

He made his choice.

Now, I'm making mine for the sake of my baby.

Ricca nods, her gaze moving from me to the boxes. "I understand. It's just hard to watch you go through this, you know?"

"I know." Digging my fingernails into my palms, I stand up straight, trying to quell the fear rising in my chest. "But I have to do this for me and my child."

Ricca takes a step into the room, her eyes scanning the boxes. "Do you need any help?"

I shake my head before pausing. "Actually, could you help me with one thing?"

"Of course," she replies without hesitation.

I walk over to my nightstand and pull out an envelope. *One last letter.* "I need you to give this to Lucas after I'm gone."

She takes the envelope from me, turning it over in her hands. "What is it?"

"He'll understand," I say, my voice barely a whisper.

Ricca nods, her dark eyes brimming with unshed tears. "I'll take care of it."

"I'm going to run this out to my car… back in a few minutes." I turn toward the door with a box. As I leave the room, the sound of Ricca folding down the box's lid echoes in my mind.

It's time to let go and move forward.

This is for the best—the mantra I had been repeating over and over again since I made this decision.

I'd gotten lucky. A former colleague of Presley's had been looking for a live-in nanny. While the job is in Outer Banks, North Carolina, distance really doesn't matter as long as I can get away from California. After an over-the-phone interview this morning and Presley's glowing recommendation, she'd offered me the job even when I told her I'm pregnant. In fact, she was excited at the idea that her kids would have a playmate. How I could be so lucky to find this position had to be graced by the spirits above, giving me the perfect situation. The idea that my baby can still have the sand and sea I love made the choice easier. She doesn't need me there for two weeks, but while driving solo, I want to give myself as much time as possible to decompress and safely make the drive.

I deposit the box in my car. As I shut the trunk, I hear Ricca yelling inside the house. Without a second thought, I bolt for the door.

"Ricca?" I call out.

She comes from her bedroom, three bags in her hand, including my brother's go bag. Eyes wild in terror.

"What's going on?"

"Jude texted me," she pants. "Panic button code word. Get a bag packed. We have to go." Ricca brushes past me.

"Go where?" I call after. "I don't understand what's going on!" I chase after her.

She wildly tosses the bags into the back of her SUV. "We have to go to the safe house. *Now*," she says, slamming the trunk shut. "It's not safe here anymore."

"What? Who's after us?"

"I don't know, but Jude wouldn't have used the panic code if it wasn't serious."

"Is this like a lockdown?" I'd experienced one of those when Presley and I'd sought the club's help.

"No! Go get your shit. We have to get Asher from school."

I rush inside, grabbing one of the bags I'd packed for my move that had my essentials, stuffing my cell phone charger and my prenatal vitamins in with my clothes.

I head for the door, locking it behind me as Ricca jumps in the driver's seat and starts the engine. I'm barely in the passenger seat when Ricca reverses the car, and we zoom out of the driveway.

"Yes, it's a family emergency. I'm coming to get him right now," she demands into her phone. "Have him ready to go."

My heart is pounding so hard I can barely breathe. We wind our way through the streets of the upscale neighborhood, and I can't help but feel a sense of dread growing inside me.

"Has something happened?"

"I don't know," she admits. "Jude told me we need to get to the safe house if I ever received his codeword. No questions asked. Just grab the bags and go."

"Where are we going?"

She swerves around the corner, and the passenger side tires feel as if they lift off the road.

"A cabin. That's where we meet them." Ricca's voice is steady, and I am grateful for her calm demeanor. I have no idea what's happening, but Ricca has been in the clubs for years. She knows what to do.

I nod, trying to fight back the tears forming in my eyes. "Okay."

"We're going to be okay," she reassures me, placing a hand on my arm.

She takes a hard right. Asher's school is coming up fast ahead of us. She skids into the parking lot and is out of the car before I can ask another question. She's gone only a few minutes before she's jogging out with him, confusion etched on his poor face.

"What's happening?" he asks as she ushers him in the back seat. Ricca fires back a generic answer before turning her attention back to the road. She takes side streets, avoiding the main roads until we begin to climb into the mountains.

We drive in silence, the tension palpable in the air. We finally arrive at the safe house, which is a large cabin in the woods. Several cars are already parked outside, but we see no motorcycles.

We gather our belongings and head to the door when it cracks open, and a gun barrel peeks through the space. One of the prospects stares out behind it before it lowers, and they open the door for us. Once done, he takes up his post again, his gun still in his hand.

We step inside, the smell of pine and cedar wood filling my nostrils. Presley, Dani, and Darcy are huddled on a set of couches in a room off the entrance, speaking softly between each other. The kids are in the other room, a television on to keep them occupied. Raze's son is holding Dani's little boy on the couch.

Asher speeds off toward the other kids.

"What's happening?" I ask as Ricca and I join them.

"I don't know, but we'll be safe here. They'll contact us when it's safe to return," Darcy responds.

I nod, feeling completely overwhelmed. I thought leaving Lucas and California would be the hardest thing I'd ever done, but now I realize I was completely unprepared for whatever is happening. All I can do is pray everything will be okay.

As I take a seat on the couch next to the other women, I can't help but feel like I'm in a daze. My thoughts are racing, and fear grips me tightly. We sit in silence for what feels like hours, each of us lost in our thoughts until finally, the sound of motorcycles is heard.

Minutes later, Raze steps into the room with a stern expression etched on his face.

Darcy rises, crossing the room to embrace her husband, soot and blood streaking his face.

"What happened?"

"We were raided."

"By who?" Dani asks.

"Homeland Security."

My heart drops in my chest as Raze's words sink in. The clubhouse was raided? What does that mean for us? For the club? For Lucas? My mind races with questions, but before I can even voice any of them, Raze continues, "We got word at the last minute and were able to get everyone out before they got to us. But the damage is done. The clubhouse is gone… burned to the fucking ground."

Presley's eyes widen in shock, and I can see the worry etched on Dani's face. Darcy looks pale, and even Ricca seems shaken.

"What do we do now?" I whisper, feeling lost and helpless.

"We lay low for a little while. Let things calm down," Raze says, his voice gentle but firm. "We'll figure something out. But right now, we need to focus on keeping everyone safe."

More motorcycles arrive, each club member making a beeline to their wives. Ricca runs to Jude, taking him in her arms. They hold each other like they're the only people in the room. Ricca's eyes are closed, and her grip on Jude is tight. I give them space for a few minutes before I make my approach when I note they're all here.

All except one.

"Where is he?" I ask my brother. "Is Lucas on his way?"

"The rat isn't our problem anymore," he sneers.

"The rat?"

Jude's jaw clenches as he speaks, his eyes darkening with anger. "Slider was an informant for the Feds. He sold us out. He's fucking responsible for all of this."

No, that can't be possible.

He loved this club.

He loved wearing their patch.

Why would he give all that up?

Chapter 34

GINNY

MY BROTHER'S words blast through the air like shattering glass.

"It can't be true," I protest, my voice weak and pleading. "Are you certain it was him?" Despair wells up in me as my hope for a mistake dwindles.

"I am," Jude snarls. "I fucking saw it with my own eyes. He set fire to the clubhouse."

My brain spins in circles, desperately trying to decipher how this could have happened. Lucas had been distant the days before he went off with Ruby, but was that enough to drive him to burn everything he once loved?

"No way," I whisper, disbelief oozing out of me.

"It doesn't matter what you believe, Gin. I know what I saw."

V steps away from Presley, joining my brother.

"He's right, Ginny. I checked the video feeds before the Feds showed up. Slider carried gas cans into the clubhouse." He pulls up his cell, and a video begins to play. I watch in horror as Lucas walks confidently into the clubhouse with two metal gas cans in his hand. He pauses at the back camera. His bright blue eyes peering up at the lens, displaying his betrayal in black and white before stepping inside the building.

Tears stream down my face the longer I watch. The feed cuts out a few minutes later as the red hue of flames and smoke takes over the screen before it cuts out.

"Where is he now?" I gulp, unsure I want to know the answer.

"I left him in that clubhouse to burn." My brother shifts his gaze to the floor before peering back at me.

"You did what?" I gasp.

I stare at my brother as he continues to stare at the floor, his lips pressed tightly together.

"It's done, Ginny," Jude says finally, his voice low and controlled. "I'm sorry."

My body shakes with sobs as I try to process that my brother has just admitted to leaving my ex-boyfriend to die. I want to scream at him, hit him, or do anything to make the pain go away. But I'm frozen, unable to move or speak. I knew he'd done terrible things, but to kill the father of my child, even if we aren't together anymore, seems cruel even for him.

Jude's face is hard and unyielding. "He betrayed our club, Gin. He brought the Feds to our door. There's no telling what they gleaned from the raid. They showed up as the fire was starting. This could be the end for us all."

My mind is in a fog as I try to wrap my head around everything that's happening. The man I once loved—still love if I am honest with myself—and the father of my child is gone. I can't believe he is capable of such an act, but the evidence is right there on V's cell.

Lucas burned down the clubhouse, and now he's dead at my brother's hands.

A part of me wants to scream and lash out at Jude for what he did, but another part of me knows Lucas brought this upon himself. He betrayed the club and, in doing so, put everyone's lives in danger, including mine.

Eventually, I find my voice. "What now?" I ask, wiping away the tears from my eyes.

"We lay low," Jude replies. "We need to regroup and figure out how we're going to move forward from this. If we can."

I nod, still numb from the shock. V hands me his

cell, and I watch the video again—Lucas walking into the clubhouse with the gas cans, his eyes meeting the camera.

I want to argue that Lucas is a good man and would never intentionally hurt anyone he loved, but as I replay the video in my mind, I see the conviction in his eyes. He made his choice, much like he had about our relationship, and now he was gone.

"I just heard," Presley remarks, her voice soft. "Are you okay?"

"I have no idea."

Presley draws me into a tight hug, her arms warm around my neck.

"He was the father of my child," I whisper.

"I know," she murmurs, her fingers rubbing small circles on my back. "But you can't change what happened. You have to trust that Jude did what he thought was best for the club."

"But at what cost?" I ask, my voice barely above a whisper. "How many more lives will be lost because of this?"

Presley pulls back from our embrace, looking me in the eyes. "We don't know what's going to happen, Ginny. But we can't dwell on the past. We have to focus on the future and how we can pick up the pieces after the smoke settles from all of this. You have to think about your baby."

"I know," I say, taking a deep breath. "I just need some time to process everything."

"You take all the time you need," she says, giving me one last hug before pulling away. "We'll be here for you no matter what."

With that, Presley leaves, leaving me alone with my thoughts and a deep ache in my heart. The last thing I had said to him is replaying in my mind. *Our baby deserves a better father than you.* The barb I had slung at him to make him feel the pain he inflicted on me—my version of revenge. Words I now wish I could take back. I peer down at my stomach, and the life we created together, and all I can do is cry.

The remainder of the night is a blur. The men went into an office toward the back of the cabin while the rest of us stayed in the two large living rooms. Darcy and Dani had taken most of the kids to the second floor, where they'd laid out sleeping bags for the kids in the large loft.

The guys finally emerge from their meeting, seeking solace in their wives. As most of them disperse to sleep, the prospect stationed at the front of the door stiffens and cranes his neck to the side. "Lights coming up the road," he yells.

The men move swiftly toward the windows. Raze's voice is a whip, slicing through the air as he orders us upstairs. We obey without hesitation, our feet shuffling in haste over the creaking wooden floor, racing to the loft where our children lay sleeping. The distant crunch of boots against gravel heralds danger, and Raze moves with purpose, positioning V and Jude out of sight on either side of the door as he takes his place directly behind it, ready to pounce. A loud knock reverberates through the cabin, and we all hold our breath.

Raze's voice echoes through the wooden halls like thunder as he snarls, "Identify yourself."

I hear the voice, barely audible, and my heart drops.

It's not possible.

It can't be.

Cautiously, I creep to the edge of the loft for a better look and see a lone figure in the doorway. His hands are empty, and he moves slowly, his face illuminated by the moonlight.

My heart races, disbelief warring with relief.

He is alive.

Lucas is alive.

Chapter 35

SLIDER

"HONEY, I'M HOME," I joke as V jerks me inside the cabin, the door slamming shut behind me.

"How the fuck are you alive?" Ratchet roars. He steps toward me with his fists balled at his hips, ready to strike me down like a viper sizing up his prey. "I left you for dead."

"Should have hit me harder, asshole."

Ratchet snorts derisively, clearly unconvinced. He looks like he wants to punch me, and I can see the muscles in his arms bulging as he prepares himself for a fight.

But then V steps forward, placing a hand on Ratchet's shoulder. "Easy, Ratch," he says in a calm voice.

Raze steps forward, and his eyes narrow as he

considers my words. "Did anyone follow you here?" he demands.

I shake my head.

"No one saw me leave Doc's."

Ratchet's mouth falls agape, his glare shifting between Raze and me.

"You good?"

"Broken nose, second-degree burns, and a couple of loose teeth, thanks to Ratch, but otherwise, fine."

Ratchet, Tyson, and Thor all look ready to pounce at any moment. I raise my hands in surrender, knowing that my life hangs on a slim thread as Thor lurches forward. The rest of the group circles me like hungry wolves, waiting for Raze's order to finish what Ratchet had started earlier at the clubhouse.

"Why the fuck is he here? Isn't he the rat?"

"He is," Raze declares.

"So why are you checking in on his well-being like he didn't fucking betray us to goddamn Homeland Security. That he didn't burn down our fucking clubhouse."

"Because I knew." I can feel the weight of the group's attention shifting toward me, their eyes brimming with suspicion and hatred. But Raze continues, his voice low and steady.

"You fucking knew?" Tyson snarls. "This whole

fucking time, you knew he was feeding intel to Homeland Security."

"I did," he admits.

"And you couldn't clue the rest of us in?" Irons fires back.

"For the record, I also knew." V raises his hand, a smirk on his face. "Though, I only found out because Slider here is shit at hiding hidden cameras and didn't think about the fact I have an alert system set up in my office for motion."

"It's true." I shrug. The motion causing the wounds on my face to sting, and I wince. "But, Raze knew before that. I was in over my head and couldn't find a way to save Ginny and protect the club."

The room grows quiet as the group processes this information.

My heart pounds in my chest, unsure of the outcome.

"Why didn't you clue in the rest of us? I'm the fucking VP, and I didn't know."

"They had eyes on me. I couldn't take the risk they'd figure out the tables had been turned until everything was in place. It had to be believable for what was at stake." I take a deep breath, steadying myself for what's to come.

"Which was?"

"My deal with the agent in charge was to give

them what they wanted, but in exchange, they'd leave Ginny alone."

Ratchet's fists slowly unfurl from their tight grip, but the glint in his eyes tells me he's still ready to fight at a moment's notice.

"What do you mean they'd leave my sister alone?"

"They used her as leverage. The day the agent approached me, he threatened her. He had someone following her. Had I not agreed to the deal, he'd have killed her right then and there at Asher's soccer game."

"Ward," Thrasher hisses.

"I'm assuming so," I shrug. "I had to make a split-second decision… the club or her. I chose her."

I peer up to the loft where Ginny's beautiful face peeks over the edge. Shock registers on her face before she shifts back out of sight.

"You put us all in the crosshairs for her, his fucking sister," Irons snarls. "Our club. Our families. Our goddamn livelihood."

"I didn't have a choice," I try to explain, but he cuts me off with a sharp motion of his hand.

"You always have a fucking choice," he snarls.

"Then what would you have done?" I retort, feeling my anger bubbling to the surface.

"Would you have let Ratchet's sister and the

fucking love of my life die just to stay loyal to the club?"

Irons steps forward, his eyes blazing with rage. I can see him gearing up for a fight, and I brace myself for impact. But before he can lay a hand on me, Raze intervenes, stepping between us with his arms raised in a placating gesture. "Enough," he says firmly. "We need to focus on the bigger picture here."

"And what's that?" Irons demands. "He passed information to Homeland Security. How much of a bigger picture do you fucking need?"

"He passed the information I provided him," V admits. "Tantalizing enough to wet their lips but nothing they could use against us in court. Information that will lead nowhere fast."

"There's no way for you to know that. I know you are an alleged super hacker, but we're talking about the government here. They probably have a thousand people like you on the payroll."

"First off, there is only one me," V scoffs. "Back to your question, the flash drive used to provide them with said information had a little surprise attached… a virus crafted by yours truly. The moment he connected it to his government-issued laptop and removed my kindergarten-grade encryption, my virus took root." V giggles. "And when he connected to the government network or VPN, he activated it to spread to every single computer connected to that very same network, giving me full and open access to their archives, including…" he trails off. Hands flare in front of him to coax someone else to guess, but he scoffs when no one takes the bait. "The file on the club, our ranks, and our families. You had a very lovely mug shot, Thrasher. I saved a copy of it for you."

"You did all that?" Hero quips, surprise written on his face.

"I did." He smiles. "All our records are safely tucked away in my off-site location, and Smith has nothing on us. I made sure of that."

"What about hard copies? He'd have those, wouldn't he?"

"Probably, but…" he smiles, "… I also found his home address and the demons in his closet."

"What did you do?" Thrasher gapes.

"Let's just say… Smith isn't as squeaky clean as he portrays himself to be."

"Do I even want to know?" Hero asks.

V shakes his head. "Not if you don't want to lock your little girls away for the rest of their lives, man. Dude's a predator. A careful predator who should be getting a visit anytime now from the FBI after the anonymous tip I sent in with loads of evidence to back it up."

"So, Smith's gone?"

"For the next twenty to thirty years, yes. He won't have a badge to protect him when he does get out, and that's a *big if*. Law enforcement doesn't tend to do well behind bars, especially in Gen Pop."

"Remind me never to piss off this guy," Irons thumbs at V.

"A wise decision." V winks.

The tension in the room dissipates as V's revelation sinks in. The group exchanges looks of disbelief and gratitude, realizing they have only narrowly avoided a disaster.

"I owe you one," Raze says, offering a handshake to V.

"Don't mention it," V replies with a wave of his hand. "It was just a little fun for me. A little payback too. Their dossier on me was somewhat insulting, truthfully."

"So what do we do about him?" Irons declares. The sights return to me and what I've

done. "He's still a rat."

"Ratchet?" Raze looks over to him, silently asking for his input.

Ratchet's jaw clenches, his eyes flickering between the group and me. "I can't speak for the club, but as far as I'm concerned, Slider is still Slider. My sister is alive because of him. I may hate the son of bitch right now, but I can't disagree with his decision."

"Feelings mutual, asshole." I nearly died because of him. Had V and Raze not circled back to find me when I didn't make it to the rendezvous point, I'd have gone up in smoke as Agent Smith thinks I did.

"That asshole needs to pay for what he's done," Tyson growls. "There has to be some kind of punishment."

"You're right," Raze nods, his eyes narrowing as he turns to me. "But there's a difference between a rat and a collaborator. Slider's actions may have saved Ginny's life and the club's future. We owe him that much." He steps forward, looking at all of us. "My father built this club from the ground up. While the founders had good intentions, greed took over. The shit he did, the lives he bought and sold, and the drugs perverted the bylaws we are supposed to live by. There was so much blood in that clubhouse that if anyone looked hard enough, there would be reason to lock us all up just for wearing our colors."

Raze strips his cut from his back, showing us the patch we all wore.

"Slider may have made a shit decision, one fueled by his dick rather than his brain, but in the end, he gave me what I'd been looking for so long... a clean slate and a chance for us all to hit the reset button and become the club the founders had intended us to be." Raze steps toward me. "Slider, what you did was wrong. I cannot and will not take away what happened because of it."

"I understand." I tug my cut off gingerly from my shoulder. The warm leather creaks under my grasp, and I hold it out toward Raze, relinquishing my colors.

"Did I ask for your cut?"

"No."

"Then why are you giving it to me?"

"Because…" I give him a tight smile, "… I want the chance to start over. To do right by the club, my brothers, and my family. And most importantly, because of her." I glance up toward the loft, where Ginny's face lingers again, unshed tears in her eyes. "I'm not leaving the club, Raze. I'm not turning my back on my brothers or our way of life, but I need to make things right. And if that means walking away from the club for a while to sort myself out, then that's what I'll do. I owe it to Ginny."

Raze looks at the cut in his hand before handing it back to me. "I don't accept your resignation. Time you can have, but this belongs to you." I peer down at it as he lays it back into my hand.

"Thank you," I mutter, returning my cut over my shoulders.

The group begins to disperse, but Ratchet lingers by my side.

"I can't forgive you for what you did," he says, his tone cold. "But I understand why you did it."

I nod, grateful for the faint glimmer of understanding. It's more than I had hoped for.

"Sorry for leaving you for dead," he mutters.

"I kind of deserved it." I smile.

"Yeah, you did." Ratchet shoves his hands into his pockets and makes to leave. "But if any of the guys give you shit for this, let me know. I'll make sure they understand."

I nod, grateful for the offer. "Thanks, man. I appreciate it…" I pause, unsure if I should ask what's swirling inside me, but I do it anyway. "I'd like to talk to Ginny."

Ratchet looks at me with a raised eyebrow. "She's been through enough, Slider."

"I know," I reply quickly. "I want to apologize and let her know I'm going to make things right."

"If you're going to do that, then you need to leave her alone. Let her heal and move on. Don't drag her back into this mess. She's leaving in a few days and has a real chance to get away from this place. Don't hinder it."

"I won't," I promise. "I just need to say this one thing to her, and then I'll back off."

Ratchet hesitates for a moment before nodding his head. "Fine. But keep it short."

Quickly, I make my way toward the staircase leading up to the loft. As I climb the stairs, my heart races with anticipation. I haven't seen Ginny since she left me outside the clubhouse. The sting of her slap still burns on my flesh.

When I reach the top of the staircase, I see Ginny sitting on the edge of the bed in one of the bedrooms to the left of the loft, filled with the other ladies and kids, staring out the window. Her back is to me, and for a moment, I hesitate. But then I take a deep breath and step forward into the room.

"Ginny," I say softly. She turns toward me, and I instantly see the pain in her eyes. "I just want to say that I'm sorry. For everything."

She doesn't say anything for a moment, and I feel my palms becoming sweaty, but then she speaks, "I don't know if I can ever forgive you," she says quietly.

"I understand," I reply. "And I don't expect you to. I fucked up. I should have told you what was going on in the first place, but I didn't know how to tell you without putting you in danger." I pause, unsure if there's anything else I can say.

But then Ginny stands up and steps closer to me,

her gaze still hard. "No more lies. No more bullshit. Did you fuck her?"

I shake my head. "Nothing happened with Ruby."

"Then what did I see?"

"You saw a man, desperate to keep you safe. If you'd have stayed, Smith would have used you against me. I couldn't let that happen… not after finding out you're pregnant."

"You sacrificed our love to save me?"

"Yes. I'd do it a million times over to keep you both safe."

Ginny takes a deep breath, and I watch her fighting the tears that fight to break through.

"I love you, Ginny. I couldn't let anything happen to you, not if I could help it. I had to make a decision, and I chose you."

Ginny stills in front of me, allowing the tears to break through their dam and stream down her face. "I'm still so angry at you," she whispers.

"I know. I'm sorry."

She steps closer, and I smell her shampoo as she moves. I reach out and wipe away a stray tear from her cheek.

"I'm leaving, Lucas. This doesn't change that."

"I know," I admit. I pull her into my arms, feeling

her embrace one last time. She sobs against my shoulder. "I know."

Letting her go may be the hardest decision I've made, but it's the right one.

I step back and give her a tight smile.

"Go and be happy, Ginny," I whisper, hoping she knows what I'm trying to say beneath my words. "That's all I can ask."

Chapter 36

GINNY

"ARE you sure this is what you want?" Jude asks, staring at the boxes still next to the door that should have been in North Carolina right now being unpacked.

"I'm not sure of anything anymore, Jude. I was so sure I wanted to leave, but I can't seem to get in my car and leave California behind."

Thankfully, Mrs. Scott had been more than understanding when I'd explained an emergency had come up. She'd been able to retain her current nanny for a few more weeks until she returned to college, giving me the time I needed to sort out the mess swirling inside my head.

Jude takes a deep breath and places a comforting hand on my shoulder. "Leaving isn't always easy, especially when you've built a life here. But remember why you wanted to leave in the first place... all the reasons that brought you to this decision."

Reasons that, until recently, I'd been so convicted in my decision. I was so sure this was what I wanted until I learned the truth and realized how much Lucas had sacrificed to keep me safe.

Yes, he'd hurt me—cut me straight to the quick, shattering my heart and every ounce of trust I had in him in the process, but he broke us to save me and our baby. Anger brews to life inside me when I think about seeing him and Ruby together, even knowing now it wasn't as it seemed.

"What if I made a mistake?" I whisper, feeling the tears starting to build behind my eyes. "What if staying here is a mistake?"

Jude's expression softens, and he pulls me into a hug. "It's okay. There's no shame in changing your mind. You have to do what feels right for you," he says, his voice soothing and warm. "The idea of you being so far away isn't what I want for you, but it's your life. Your decision. You've earned that chance."

"I know, but it's hard to let go of everything, even the damn palm trees outside my window."

Jude chuckles lightly, trying to ease the tension. "I understand, but sometimes letting go is the only way to move forward, and who knows what new adventures await you in North Carolina."

"Maybe you're right." I sigh.

"I'm older than you, so of course, I'm always fucking right."

I elbow my brother in his ribs. He tips over, feigning injury.

"Don't be a pussy, Jude. I've seen a pillow hit you harder than that," I fire back.

He reaches for a pillow from my bed behind me and smacks me in the face with it.

"Hey," I exclaim.

"What? I saw a bug. A big one."

"Asshole." I roll my eyes as a large smile forms on my lips.

"It's nice to see you smile again."

A pregnant pause settles between us. The question I have been dying to ask him lingers in my mind before I finally garner enough courage to ask, "How is he?"

"Do you really want to know?"

I nod. "I do."

"He's staying with V, last I heard." Jude takes a deep breath before slowly releasing it. "He's a mess. The fucker has been moping around. He asks about you, you know? Every time I see him. Annoying as shit."

I raise an eyebrow in surprise and say, "Really?"

"Yeah, he wants to make sure you're all right," Jude says in awe, shaking his head. "Actually, he gave me something for you."

Jude pulls an envelope from his pocket and hands it to me.

"What's this?" I ask, peering down at it.

"He gave this to me to send to you since he doesn't know you're still here. I'm not sure if you want it, but I can at least say with a clear conscience that it was delivered safely."

I take the envelope hesitantly, my fingers tracing the edges lightly. I can only imagine what might be inside.

"I'll leave you to it. Ricca's picking up pizza later if you want anything. Just text her your order."

"I will." I smile.

Jude shoves off my bed, heading out the door and down the hallway, leaving me with the letter. I can't stop myself from slowly tearing off the edge of the envelope and unfolding the letter inside. My heart instantly stops at the sight of his familiar handwriting, and I can almost hear his deep voice whispering against my ear.

Ginny,

I know I said I could let you go,

but we both know how much of a shit liar I am.

I can't help but wonder where you are right now. If you're safe. If you can feel our baby growing inside you. How much I would have loved to be there when you felt its first kick.

While I can't be there in person, I want you to know I intend to support our baby even from a distance. I set up an account. Jude has the details. Use it as you see fit. It's yours for both of you should you ever need it.

I meant what I said, Gin. I want you to be happy. I want you to raise our baby to be strong like their mother. Find someone who can give you the life you both deserve. Find it, and hold onto as much as I hold onto the memory of you in my arms.

You're worth every single thing you ever dreamed of. Don't be scared of taking a chance. No matter what, Gin.

I love you both until the end.

Lucas

And suddenly, my heart knows what I have to do. I had to know.

I have to be certain I'm not making a huge mistake.

Passing my brother in the kitchen, I exit the house with Lucas' letter still in my hand. I hop into my car, the destination clear in my mind.

The house comes into view at the crest of the hill near the base of the mountain.

My heart shudders when I exit the car, my shaky legs leading me to the front door. I raise my fist to knock, but the door swings open before I can. Lucas stands there, his eyes never leaving mine. No words are exchanged, only a long, lingering embrace. With the emotions bubbling to the surface, I take a step back, regaining some semblance of my composure.

"You didn't leave."

"I didn't." I shake my head.

My mouth is dry, my palms clammy. I take a deep breath, gathering my nerves before speaking, "I'm here because I need to know. I don't know if I made the right decision, and I need to know if I'm ready to move on… or if I'm meant to stay."

Lucas gently holds my hands, lightly squeezes

them, and takes a deep breath, the weight of the world on his shoulders.

"You know what you want, Ginny. It's always been in your heart. Follow that." He gives me a small, bittersweet smile. "And if that means staying with me, then I'm all yours."

I can't help but smile back, the feeling of home filling my body. I let go of my fear, squeezing his hand tightly before nestling my head against his shoulder.

"I'm all yours," I whisper. I don't know when I forgave him, but deep down, I know I already have.

He nods and pulls me into his arms. "To the ends of the earth, Gin," he whispers, pressing his forehead to mine. "Always fucking yours. I have been from the start."

Our embrace breaks, his hand still firmly in mine.

As I gaze out at the sunset, I smile.

Everything is going to be all right.

"Let's do this together," I say softly.

"Together, Gin. You, me, and our baby," he replies, placing his hand on my belly. When his lips press to mine, I know that no matter what life throws at us, together, we can survive.

Us against the fucking world.

Epilogue

SLIDER

ONE YEAR LATER

Raze steps in front of our club, a broad smile barely hidden beneath his gray beard. The new building is shining behind him like a brand-new penny in the California summer sun.

It has been a long year without a permanent home for the club. We'd done our best, focusing on what we could rebuild while the slow process of building the clubhouse trudged on.

Our security business has flourished. Between heated political campaigns and Hollywood, our schedule has been jam-packed to the point we called in several guys from other chapters to help us out. The additional help allowed us to legitimize the club, garage, and other businesses we've been picking up along the way. We are slowly taking back our community one day at a time, protecting it as we had always intended to do before our past brothers got lost along the way.

"Welcome to your new home, boys," Raze says with a grin, gesturing to the building behind him. He raises his hand in a welcoming gesture, and I can't help but feel relief wash over me. The familiar sight of the clubhouse, the sound of motorcycles rumbling in the distance, and the scent of leather fill my senses.

It is good to be back.

The old clubhouse we had been using was rundown and cramped. Even though those old walls held so many memories of our club's history, that history needed to be erased so we don't repeat those mistakes again.

In its place, on the very foundation where our club had been forged, our new building now stands. It is everything we could have dreamed of and more. The outside is modern with sleek lines and windows filling in the open spaces. It is like a fortress, assuring our safety and providing a feeling of power untainted by our past with enough room to cover our growing ranks.

It's our future in physical form and the legacy we will leave behind for our kids and members after we're gone.

With the old clubhouse and his leverage gone, Smith hasn't reared his ugly head again. Partly because of the twenty-nine-year sentence he was issued after the FBI raided his house and found out his dirty, little child-porn secret V had uncovered. We won't be seeing him for a very long time.

Homeland Security hadn't come knocking back on our doors either. On top of the fact we'd managed to outwit them and destroy the evidence against the club, the virus V had encrypted on that flash drive had taken hold of their mainframe. A year later, he's still wreaking havoc in their systems for fun. It's his new favorite pastime if you ask him, outside of being the fucking weirdest girl dad to their new baby girl, Leia. The amount of pink, glitter, and tulle he's been buying would have you questioning a lot of things about him, but fuck, you can't deny he loves her. Though Presley may not approve of his new cosplay idea he's been showing off for his planned family costumes for the four of them for Comic-Con.

"Ready to check it out?" I ask Ginny.

Our little boy, Dutton Jude or DJ as we've been calling him, sleeps soundly against her chest. Only the wisps of his dark hair, like his mother's, peek out from under the wrap securing him to her body. Our miracle made real. I'd nearly lost both during his birth.

Ginny had gone into labor eight weeks early as we were moving into our condo. The emergency C-section and the skillful hands of her doctor are the only reasons why both are here with me after Ginny coded on the table. Three emergency surgeries later to remove her uterus after a massive hemorrhage, she came back to me, and DJ spent two months in the NICU before we got to bring him home.

While more kids may not be possible for us, it doesn't matter. They are enough for me. We've been through a lot, but it's worth the sacrifice we all made to be where we are now.

Raze leads our club and families through a set of double doors, revealing the main hall. It's like stepping into a dream. The floor is polished concrete beneath our feet, with a bar along one wall. A common area takes up a corner of the room, with lights suspended from the ceiling.

As we make our way to the back of the building, my heart races with excitement. I can only imagine what the others are feeling, the anticipation practically palpable in the air. And then, we step into the room that has been the reason for the building's construction. The room has been meticulously designed to be both functional and beautiful.

"The War Room," Raze declares, his voice echoing through the space. The room is massive, with walls made of exposed brick and a high ceiling adorned with chandeliers. But it's the massive table in the center of the room that draws everyone's attention. The table is made of dark wood and surrounded by comfortable chairs, each emblazoned with the club's insignia.

A sense of pride washes over me as we continue the tour.

We've come so far and fought so hard to get here. And now, we have a place of our own, a place where we can be a family again.

Ginny walks over to one of the chairs, her eyes wide with wonder. I see the gears turning inside her head, and a grin spreads across her lips.

"We're really back," she says softly, looking around the room. "Back where we belong."

"Yes, baby, we are. We're finally home."

Heaven's Rejects MC Series

Heaven Sent

Angels and Ashes

Absolution

Lies and Illusions

Resolution

Song List

"Just Pretend" - Bad Omens

"Stay" - Black Stone Cherry

"Bring Me To Life" - Evanescence

"How You Remind Me" - Nickelback

"The Dairy of Jane" - Breaking Benjamin

"Lips of an Angel" - Hinder

"Fake It" - Seether

"Hero" - Skillet

"Never Enough" - Five Finger Death Punch

"Careless Whisper" - Seether

"Simple Man (Rock Version)" - Shinedown

"Save Yourself" by My Darkest Days

"Zombie" - The Cranberries

"Broken (featuring Amy Lee)" - Seether

"Hollow Man" - Rev Theory

"The Sound of Silence" - Disturbed

Acknowledgements

It's hard to consider that one chance trip to Disneyland would give me the inspiration to write the Heaven's Rejects MC. It's fitting really to write the final "The End" nearly eight years to the day that Heaven Sent was published. In closing the final chapter of the Heaven's Rejects MC series, I am overwhelmed with gratitude for the incredible journey this has been. To all my readers and supporters who have embarked on this ride with me, your unwavering enthusiasm and encouragement have meant the world to me.

I owe immeasurable thanks to my dedicated team and beta readers, whose insights and feedback shaped this series into what it is today. Your commitment and passion for the story were instrumental in bringing the characters and their world to life.

A special shout-out goes to my family and friends who patiently endured my writing process, listened to my plot ideas at odd hours, and provided endless bottles of Coke. Your belief in me sustained my creative spirit even when I thought my muse had packed its shit and left.

Lastly, to my loyal readers who have stuck with me from the beginning, your dedication is the heart and soul of this series. It's been an incredible honor to share this world with you, and I hope the conclusion is everything you've hoped for.

As I pen the words "The End" to the Heaven's Rejects MC series, I do so with a heart full of gratitude and a tear in my eye. While this chapter may be closing, I'm excited to embark on new adventures with you in the future.

Until then, ride safe, keep the wind at your back, and always remember the love and loyalty we've forged through these pages.

Meet Avelyn

Avelyn Paige is a Wall Street Journal and USA TODAY bestselling author of romantic suspense and motorcycle club romance. She lives in a small town in Indiana with her husband and five fuzzy kids.

When she's not writing, Avelyn spends her days working as a cancer research scientist. Avelyn has been an avid reader her entire life, and it wasn't until losing her father in 2015 that she started turning all those ideas in her head into stories. She hasn't looked back since.

Join Avelyn's Reader Group: Avelyn's Angels

ALSO BY AVELYN PAIGE

The Heaven's Rejects MC Series

Heaven Sent

Angels and Ashes

Sins of the Father

Absolution

Lies and Illusions

The Black Hoods MC

Dark Protector

Dark Secret

Dark Guardian

Dark Desires

Dark Destiny

Dark Redemption

Dark Salvation

Dark Seduction

The Bastard Boilers MC

Property of Azrael